HLW

12.10.16

1 6 MAR

GW00482340

Please return this book on or before the date shown
above. To renew go to www.essex.gov.uk/libraries,
ring 0845 603 7628 or go to any Essex library.

DS12 4005

Essex County Council

30130503266050

ISBN: 978-1-927477-93-9

Prologue

Thursday, August 18, 2016—the town of St. Anthony, Canada

The night sky was filled with shooting stars. There weren't many residents here, in the smallest town on the "wrong" side of Dinosaur Provincial Park, but the local population always swelled for the Perseid Shower Festival in August. It was dark in St. Anthony, far beyond the light pollution of any metropolis, which provided the best viewing conditions for meteor enthusiasts. The festival had been held the previous Saturday, the biggest ever, but now most of the visitors had departed.

This was the night of the full moon, the least optimal time to watch the meteors, after all. Most residents had had their fill of meteors and were watching television instead. The local bar, MacEnroe's Pub & Eatery, had closed down at midnight and the streets were empty.

By the wee hours of the morning, all four

hundred and twenty residents of St. Anthony were asleep and the meteor shower illuminated the sky unobserved. No one noticed that a single larger meteor hurtled toward the earth. It streamed white fire across the sky and crashed into the badlands not far outside of town with a thunderous crash.

Even that didn't rouse any townsfolk from their sleep.

The ball of flame rolled a distance, then stopped. The meteor was in fact a ship, a ship carrying a MindBender, the most powerful MindBender ever born in the galaxy. He had cloaked the ship in invisibility, a wasted effort since there was no one in the vicinity.

He wanted to arrive without notice.

When the ship halted, the flames were abruptly extinguished. The sphere cracked in half, revealing a seam too straight to have been naturally forged, and the lone occupant stepped out. He stretched when he stood on the ground, then surveyed his surroundings.

Didn't it figure that they'd sent him back to Earth. Troy shook his head. The sneaky bastards. The gamblers of Xanto always kept a few aces up their sleeves. He hoped this was the only surprise, but doubted it.

He was going to win, even so.

Anything he had to do was better than being executed.

Troy had never imagined he'd return to Earth, but here he stood, on terra firma once again. He studied the town and felt surprise. Not just on his home planet, but outside the town where he'd grown up.

Two surprises in as many minutes. They really were trying to stack the odds against him.

And thanks to the High Priestess of Nimue, no one would recognize him. Was that good or bad? Troy knew that no one would believe where he had been.

There were times when he didn't believe it himself. If it hadn't been for the ship—which was already decomposing—and the persistent ache in his muscles from working in the mines of the penal colony of Xanto, he might have thought he'd never left St. Anthony, that he'd just taken a walk on this night in the wilderness.

But Troy knew better. He was changed. He was bitter and he was angry. His heart had turned to stone at the injustice done to him. He had one chance to make it right, to earn his freedom, and even if they stacked *all* the odds against him, he was going to win.

Or die trying.

It had to be better than execution.

Troy had forty-eight hours in local time to succeed in his mission. Two rotations of the Earth to kill a dragon shifter princess. A simple transaction. His life for hers.

He had no idea why anyone wanted to have the princess Drakina executed, and he didn't particularly care. If he cared, he might not be able to finish the job. Caring was a luxury Troy couldn't afford.

He was here and he had a job to do. He started walking.

Earth might be less developed than the other

civilizations he'd come to know, but the planet itself wasn't bad. The temperature and humidity were pleasant, the air smelled good, and the oxygen balance was excellent. The force of gravity was a little lighter than Troy had become accustomed to, but he'd get used to it again easily enough. Out here, far from most humans, it was perfect.

Funny how he hadn't thought that when he was younger. He'd thought himself trapped and hadn't been able to get away. As he strode toward slumbering St. Anthony, Troy appreciated what he'd left behind.

He had one chance.

He had it all planned. He'd MindBend her, disarm her, and finish the mission. His gift would mean that he'd be able to anticipate her, even read her mind. Troy would do whatever he had to do, and not regret it one bit.

He wasn't going back to Xanto.

The gift that had gotten him off this planet would save his butt now.

When Troy reached the perimeter of St. Anthony, he was glad to be unobserved. The sight of the familiar jolted him with emotions he didn't need to feel and he fought to be impassive again. But the Grand Hotel was just the way he remembered. MacEnroe's Pub & Eatery where Ruby used to give him extra fries. Old man Wilcox's garage, where he'd left his beloved Harley. His parents' graves were in the cemetery behind the church on the far side of town. He remembered those funerals all too well. He'd gone to school over to the left and turned, haunted by happier memories. He'd ridden his bike down that trail and out to the badlands.

Hunting dragons.

Some things didn't change.

Home was home, even if he couldn't stay.

Troy felt the hairline crack in the surface of his heart like a wound and set his jaw. It was all part of the game. They were deliberately messing with him, trying to undermine his abilities with sentiment.

The gamblers of Xanto weren't counting on Troy's desire to survive.

He *would* win.

"I won't do it," Drakina insisted, folding her arms across her chest. She was in the royal audience chamber of Incendium's main palace, confronting her parents yet again. The chamber was large and luxuriously appointed, even the walls touched with gilding. The floor was a mosaic pattern that was actually a puzzle, made of inlaid stone from every territory governed by the monarchy of Incendium. The power and expanse of her father's domain was evident in every detail of his palace and, as leader of one of the most advanced societies in the galaxy, the claw of the King of Imperium reached far across the universe.

His influence within his family, however, was often challenged.

Usually by his oldest daughter, Drakina.

Drakina stood tall before her father, undaunted by his glower of disapproval. Her eleven sisters hovered behind her, watching avidly.

Twenty-two royal advisors and astrologers hovered around the perimeter of the room, also observing, but they were more wary of the king's wrath than his brood of daughters. There were already sparks in the air, leaping between father and daughter.

"I won't," Drakina repeated. Sparks shot from the tips of her long red hair, circling the pair like brilliant butterflies before they fell to the floor and blackened to ash.

"Of course, you will," Ouros countered. Drakina's father was regal and commanding, but he *had* been king of the realm for five centuries. Getting his own way had become a habit.

It was also Drakina's habit. Oldest of the brood, she was the most stubborn.

"It's your destiny, dear," her mother said, her tone soothing. "You can't escape a prophecy."

"That's what you said the last time," Drakina replied tartly. "It's your own fault I don't believe it now."

Her mother shifted shape in her agitation and fluttered at the reminder of the fiasco. In her dragon form, Ignita was a thousand hues of mauve and pale blue, as ethereal as a morning mist. She liked to disguise her will of iron behind her feminine wiles. "There was no need to create a diplomatic incident," she said.

"I tried saying no," Drakina replied. "That didn't work."

Her mother's expression became exasperated. "Well, we had signed the betrothal agreement."

"You should have asked me first."

"You are a royal princess!" her mother cried. "No one asks royal princesses who they wish to marry."

"They should," one of Drakina's sisters whispered. It was impossible to tell which one, but Drakina would have bet it was Gemma.

She'd been quiet since her betrothal to Prince Urbanus of Regalia had been announced. Drakina would have bet that her sister was planning something. Revenge? Rebellion? With Gemma it was always hard to guess.

Their father heard the words. Drakina could tell by the way his eyes narrowed.

"Did you ask me first before *you* responded?" He glowered at his disobedient daughter, clearly seeing that she was sowing dissent in the ranks. Drakina could see that he, too, was on the cusp of shifting. Her father changed shape to ensure that he got his way. She bounced a little on her toes, ready to go one-to-one over this and more sparks took flight from her hair. "No one says that destiny is always easy, Drakina," he said, as if trying to make peace. She wasn't fooled. He didn't believe in doing anything against his own will, either.

"You must have *needed* that humiliation," her mother argued. "There must have been a point."

Her mother had been talking to the astrologers again, it was clear.

"Obviously, she's much more humble," her youngest sister Peri whispered behind her. Peri was the mischievous one and the pretty one. The other sisters giggled and jostled for a better view.

The results of Drakina's defiance were often spectacular.

Their father's nostrils flared and a small puff of

smoke emanated from one of them. "Drakina did not learn from the experience, because she was too impatient!" he declared. "Too impetuous."

"Too hungry," added a sister. Again the words came from their ranks but couldn't be readily attributed to any of them. *Flammara*, Drakina thought. *The outspoken one.*

Ouros seethed that the defiance was spreading.

"I don't want anything to do with destiny," Drakina argued. "I just want to choose for myself."

"Then think of this as a way to achieve that," her father countered. He sounded reasonable but his eyes were glittering. "Do this for the kingdom, then you can do whatever you want." He held up a finger. "One concession and your life will be yours."

Drakina regarded her father with suspicion. Ouros did have a reputation as a slippery negotiator. "How exactly would that work?" she demanded, hearing all the skepticism of a wyvern much younger than herself in her own tone.

Her father smiled, showing a vast collection of teeth. He was doing that annoying thing again, the one that really irked Drakina, of hovering on the cusp of change. If she looked at him with one eye, he was in his human form. With the other, she could see his majestic dragon form, all imperial blue and gold. With both eyes open, the view was troubling. Many people agreed to whatever he requested when he did this, just to make him stop.

"This could be the last errand you do for me and for the kingdom," he said smoothly, sounding like the voice of reason. "Do this and I will never ask another thing of you."

"I don't believe it. You're exiling me. It's punishment."

Her father's eyes flashed and the dragon was briefly ascendant. He remained in human form with an obvious effort. His gaze bored into hers and she felt the weight of his will. "I swear it to you, daughter of mine."

Drakina averted her gaze. "Even if that's true, it's a lot to ask. It's not easy to bear a dragon shifter."

"Your father requests no more than what is natural," her mother countered. "I had *twelve* children for the sake of the kingdom. Why can't you bear just one?"

"For the sake of your kind," her father added.

"To ensure the future of all you love," her mother urged.

"To defend your home," her father added, his voice booming.

Drakina hesitated.

"What if she doesn't do it?" Callida dared to ask. She always had to know the details.

Their father flung out his arms and shifted shape, his dragon form filling the chamber. His minions flinched, cowering against the walls in anticipation of his wrath. "Then all will be lost!" he roared, sending a plume of fire at the ceiling. The architect looked worried. "Destiny will be denied, doom will befall us, and the once magnificent Kingdom of Incendium will crumble to dust!"

"As long as the prospects aren't too dire," Drakina said, unable to deny herself the opportunity to provoke her father.

He glared at her and exhaled a stream of smoke.

A chef hastened forward, obviously hoping to calm the monarch by offering a gilded tray with some confection displayed upon it. "Would you care to sample the roast cervus from Sylvawyld, my lord?"

Ouros turned upon the chef, who quivered on the spot, then the king's nostrils flared. His gaze brightened. He bent with utmost delicacy and plucked the haunch from the platter, sniffing appreciatively. He devoured it in one bite and gave the chef a gleaming smile. "Excellent," he purred. "Most excellent. You changed the spice blend. It's much better."

"Thank you, Majesty." The chef bowed and backed away from those impressive teeth. "I live to please you, Majesty."

The exchange had given Drakina time to think without being under the pressure of her father's will. When he eyed her again, she had her compromise ready. "I won't marry him," she insisted and her father chuckled that he had won the encounter.

He shifted shape, becoming the benign patriarch again. He was always so smug when he won. It made her want to bite something.

Or someone.

Preferably a crown prince from Regalia.

"You don't have to," Ouros ceded amiably. "Just take his seed and conceive the boy."

"I can just take it?" Drakina asked with new hope. "Does it matter if he survives?"

Her mother put a hand on her husband's arm and stepped forward. "Of course, it does, my dear. You must *seduce* him and let him survive, but then you can abandon him. This is romance, after all."

Drakina's suspicion rose. They were making this too easy. "Shouldn't he be my official Consort, if he's the father of the heir?"

"He doesn't need to know," her father said, dismissing the very idea.

"He's Terran," her mother whispered, which explained Ouros' attitude.

His prejudices were at work. If Destiny had twined Drakina's path with a Terran, her father wouldn't want a specimen of such an inferior species to have an official role in his court. For once, her father's attitudes were a relief.

"He's a means to an end, no more than that. We cannot evade that he is the Carrier of the Seed, but there is no need to celebrate such a truth."

For once, Drakina felt that her father's objectives and her own might dovetail nicely. Bearing one son and evading responsibility forever sounded like a good deal. She didn't really want a Consort either.

Ouros beckoned to his viceroy who turned one wall into a glowing display with a gesture. "Kraw? Could you tell Drakina more, please?"

"With greatest pleasure, Majesty." The viceroy bowed deeply to each of the royal family, which took sufficient time that Drakina found her toe tapping. Kraw must have caught a whiff of her impatience for he spoke more quickly.

Those servants who survived a long tenure in a royal household of dragon shifters tended to be those who were alert to changes of mood in their lords and ladies.

"This is the planet Earth." The display showed a blue and green planet. Drakina knew little of the place beyond her father's disdain for its occupants. At Kraw's gesture, the view closed in on a land mass. Magnification revealed an open expanse that looked quite inviting. "And here is where you will find the Carrier, in a wilderness of sorts."

Ouros made a rumble of approval. "Good for courting," he said, taking Ignita's hand in his own. She smiled at him, as they clearly recalled their own courting days.

"Is it warm?" Drakina asked, admiring the amount of room.

"Seasonally so, Highness. You will find the climate similar to the plains of Aequor, particularly at this time of year. Moderate in the days compared to our hotter zones, and cool in the evenings. It is cold in winter, but you will have departed by then."

"How soon will that be?" Drakina was drawn closer out of her infernal curiosity.

Kraw gestured to an astrologer who cleared his throat. "Currently, this hemisphere of Terra has passed the midpoint of its hottest season," the astrologer began. Drakina remembered him as one inclined to be long-winded. "Of course, their solar days and hours are of different duration than ours, due to the relative size of their sun and the diameter of Terra's orbit around that sun..."

Kraw interrupted the lecture. "If you would be so kind as to consult your assistant, Highness, I have taken the liberty of loading it with time and language converters for Terra."

"Thank you, Kraw." Drakina didn't comment that her father must have been very certain he'd get his way. She lifted the square film and tapped in her query, the conversion instantaneous and satisfactory.

"You will, of course, take an entourage to see to your comfort, and a troop of bodyguards," Ouros began.

"No," Drakina said firmly. "I go alone or not at all."

A flutter passed through the court and the astrologers took a step back.

Her father glared at her once more. "I will not see my oldest daughter imperiled..."

"I am a dragon shifter, Father. I can take care of myself."

Their gazes locked in a battle of wills once more, then Kraw cleared his throat. "If I may be so bold, Majesty, there is wisdom in the princess' suggestion. The occupants of this Earth are all of the standard biped form and size, so she will be able to ensure her own protection in her dragon form. Also, this planet is not sufficiently advanced to be shown any indication of life elsewhere in the galaxy, by interstellar law, so she would draw less attention alone."

Ouros harrumphed but conceded the point.

Drakina began to feel a prickle of excitement. An adventure alone. A seduction on a distant planet. An assignment that would see her freed from the weight of her father's claw. It couldn't get any better.

There had to be a catch.

"And this is Troy," Kraw announced with pride. "The Carrier of the Seed."

Drakina looked up with anticipation and barely managed to keep from grimacing.

There was a moment of silence in the audience

chamber.

"Are you sure?" Splendea asked in a horrified whisper.

"I'm not sure *that* genetic stock should be perpetuated," whispered Percipia.

"He might be your HeartKeeper," Peri teased and they laughed as one.

Drakina was already fighting her revulsion and wasn't even in the Carrier's presence yet. She studied the display, unable to explain why he was her destined mate. He must have been chosen to carry the seed for a reason, but she couldn't discern what it was. He was a biped, as Kraw had indicated, with the usual pairs of appendages. She checked his proportions and knew they would couple readily enough. He was muscled and fit, not unappealing in that way, but his face was enough to make her wince.

He had to be one of the ugliest creatures she'd ever seen, even for an inferior species. His brows were low and dark, his jaw was huge with a fierce underbite, and his eyes were small and glittering.

"Ewww," said Peri, perfectly expressing Drakina's own reaction.

"Don't keep him, Drakina," advised Flammara, the second youngest of the princesses. Drakina had no intention of doing so.

Maybe his appearance would make it easier to just use him for her own purposes and discard him.

She couldn't care for someone who looked like that.

She would have to close her eyes for the union.

If not the courtship.

No, there would be no courtship. It would be a

quick seduction.

Very quick.

"Your father *said* she doesn't have to keep him," their mother reminded them.

Ouros lifted his hand in his most majestic manner, and the princesses almost groaned aloud at this sign that he would tell a story. "Kraw has discovered a tale told by Terrans of one Helen of Troy. He must be named for her." Ouros beamed at his daughters. He loved stories from primitive cultures.

"What was her story, Papa?" Peri asked, no doubt because someone was expected to do so.

Ouros beamed at his youngest daughter. "Her beauty was such that when she was seized from her betrothed by his rival, a thousand ships were launched to retrieve her."

"I can see why we're sending only one," Drakina countered and her sisters giggled.

"He looks as dumb as a rock," Flammara said.

"Well, he *is* Terran," Peri reminded them. "They don't even do space travel."

"No colonies at all," Ouros confirmed with a shake of his head. "They haven't settled their own moon and it's quite close."

The astrologer provided a measurement that incited pity in all those present.

"Quite backward, I'm afraid," Ignita said with a flutter. "But you won't have to stay long, dear. Just get the Seed."

"And don't rouse any suspicion," Kraw added.

"Maybe this will be easy, Drakina," said Thalina, the sister most inclined to be sympathetic. "Maybe you'll be home again and pregnant in no time."

Maybe.

Drakina considered the image of the Carrier and wondered whether she could do this feat for her kind.

Then she saw the resolve in her father's eye and knew that she had to succeed.

How long could it take?

"I'll do it," she said. Her father's smile of satisfaction gave her a moment's doubt, as if she didn't quite have all the facts.

But her father wouldn't confess more than he had.

More importantly, Drakina had given her word, and she'd keep it.

To Terra, she would go, as soon as possible. The egg ripened within her and the time for conception was close.

The sooner she embarked on the journey, the sooner it would be done.

CHAPTER ONE

D rakina teleported after her mate, impatient to have her quest completed. She'd done her research on the planet Terra and added more local languages to her interpretor. Kraw had only loaded Mandarin but Drakina had found more possibilities. She'd rather have too much information than too little.

Kraw wouldn't be the one facing trouble if Drakina arrived unprepared.

The planet circled a distant sun, rotating as it did so, which resulted in a familiar suite of time divisions, which the Terrans called "day," "night," and "year'" The actual amount of time differed from Incendium, and Kraw's choice of conversion engine for relative time was excellent. Even having been warned of the scientific backwardness, Drakina had been shocked by her research. It would not be unlike a visit to Sylvawyld, the planet in their system that the kings of Incendium chose to keep unspoiled, to better preserve the hunting.

Drakina was further surprised that Terrans did not acknowledge the existence of shape shifters, although many of their cultures told stories of them. They called these myths and folk tales. It was most curious to tell stories of beings then deny their existence, if not delusional, but there was no accounting for regional differences. She simply had to accommodate them.

Terrans also did not believe that dragons were real. There was a startling fact. In fact, it was a kind of a joke with them, for they wrote "Here Be Dragons" on their maps in the unknown and unexplored corners of the world. Their language was filled with references to dragons, although they denied the existence of such a superior culture. Drakina found this completely irrational.

Her destined mate was Terran so clearly he could not be the Carrier because of his intellect.

She already knew it wasn't because of his appearance.

That he should be the Carrier of the Seed was a puzzle. What genetic benefit would he bring to their union? Perhaps he was particularly robust.

Perhaps she should not quibble with destiny and simply complete what had to be done with all haste. The prospect of being free of her father's dictates was more than enough incentive.

She used Kraw's coordinates and her teleport dropped her into an open area outside a settlement. To any Terran observer, she would have suddenly appeared behind a cluster of rocks. Of course, there were no observers. She'd checked. Beside the rocks was a spiked being of the slower metabolic type that Terrans called "plants." She greeted it using the galactic protocol but it didn't reply.

There was no sign, in fact, that it was aware of her or her greeting.

Was it rude, shy, or stupid? There was no way to know.

Drakina hoped her mate was a better communicator.

She hoped she was home very soon.

Drakina was in her human form, an obvious choice as a result of her research, and wore something called a "dress" with "sandals." It was shocking to her to wear a garment that left her legs exposed below the knee, but evidently this kind of lewd display was considered normal by Terrans. Drakina would have preferred to have exposed her breasts, but evidently that would have drawn attention in this curious place. Only a mate should see the thighs of a Wyvern princess, unless she chose to shift to her dragon form.

Drakina couldn't let her discomfort affect her hunt. It certainly encouraged her to hurry and have the mating behind her. She felt bold and provocative, like one of the sirens of Incendium's marketplace, and was glad her father couldn't see her like this.

Perhaps the Carrier would find the view enticing.

Drakina inhaled deeply and caught the trace of the Carrier's scent. Yes, she could smell the Seed within him. It almost beckoned to her, as if it knew its fate—as the Carrier might not.

Drakina did not care about his views. She emerged from behind the rocks and strode toward the lights of a town. His scent emanated from there. Darkness was falling and she heard night creatures on all sides. A sound emitted from the settlement, a rhythmic sound with a steady beat. It wasn't a style of music that was familiar to her, but it wasn't unpleasant. In fact, it made her want to move in rhythm with it. The music became louder as she approached the town, and she heard laughter as well. Perhaps some festivity was being celebrated.

Perhaps there would be food.

There was nothing like a teleport to make Drakina hungry.

Well, except sex. The princesses of Incendium were renowned for their appetites, after all.

After her journey, Drakina was hungry enough to eat an entire cervus, if not two. The prospect of food and sex, not necessarily in that order, quickened her steps, and made her wish she could have just shifted and flown to town.

But she could not challenge Terran assumptions. It would be irresponsible to do as much, and a violation of galactic code, on such a primitive planet as this. Sadly, restraint was not the strongest of Drakina's talents.

Surely she could keep a low profile long enough to seduce the Carrier.

Drakina followed his scent, moving with such purpose that she did draw attention. Few residents of St. Anthony had ever seen a beautiful woman stride out of the desert in high heels, much less one charging toward the bar in the Grand Hotel. If Drakina had realized how many people were watching her with curiosity, she would not have cared.

The Carrier was her target and the claiming of the Seed her goal.

There was a band playing in the bar at the Grand Hotel on Friday night and the place was comparatively busy. Troy was glad that he didn't know anyone—they wouldn't have recognized him, but he might have tripped up. The crowd was young, maybe even the children of the people he'd gone to school with, and that simplified the challenge a lot.

The lights were turned down and the music was loud. Locals crowded into the bar, buying drinks and greeting old friends. It seemed that many were celebrating the success of the recent meteor festival, which had been the biggest yet.

Troy had bought some clothes at the emporium earlier in the day. He'd visited Old Man Wilcox and bought his beloved Harley back as if he were a stranger. To Old Man Wilcox's credit, he hadn't wanted to part with the bike and insisted the rightful owner might come back.

His loyalty struck Troy in the heart.

So did the care the older man had lavished on the bike.

Finally, they struck a deal. Troy had pretended to ride out of town, but had circled back and parked the bike behind the hotel, then taken a room. It felt wrong to deceive the old man, but the truth wouldn't have been believed.

He wouldn't have believed it, if he hadn't lived it.

The mood in the bar was familiar and welcoming, enough to make Troy relax just a little. He'd missed the society of others, especially in solitary confinement, and though he was wary of relaxing too much too soon, there was something beguiling about the familiarity of this place. He watched the townspeople enjoying themselves, oblivious to other matters in the universe.

But then, that was how it should be, by galactic law.

A part of him wished that he was still as innocent, and he felt resentment that he should have been snatched away, against his will, and his life changed forever. He'd been pretty much alone even before his arrest, given the jobs he'd been given.

Troy wasn't going to indulge in regrets, though. Not now. The band was in the middle of a popular song, the crowd on their feet, dancing and singing along when a woman opened the door to the bar.

Drakina.

She couldn't have been anyone else.

When Troy had first seen Drakina's hologram, he'd been sure she was the most gorgeous woman in the galaxy. He'd assumed the hologram had been tricked up a bit, to make her look more beautiful than she was. The truth was that real life put any representation to shame. Not only was she beautiful, but she moved like a goddess. There was fire in her eyes that no representation could capture. The sight of her stole his breath away and sent a wave of astonishment through the bar.

Troy wasn't the only one who stared.

She was tall, almost as tall as him, and tanned. Her figure was slender and athletic, but there was nothing boyish about the look of her. Her breasts were lushly curved, and her waist was slim. Her hair was long and dark red, hanging past her hips in thick waves. Her eyes tilted up at the outer corners, giving her an exotic air, and her lips were full and red.

She wore a green dress that clung to her curves then fluttered at the hem, making her look gloriously feminine and sexy. Her sandals were strappy with heels that arched her feet high. There was sand on them and he wondered how far she'd walked in them. He felt the vitality emanating from her and knew there was little that would stop her.

Her eyes glittered with intelligence and he sensed the dragon restrained within her. When her gaze locked with his, it seemed particularly foolish to have a plan to deceive her much less any expectation of surviving that feat. Troy's heart skipped more than one beat.

Her beauty widened that crack in the stone of Troy's heart and sent hot blood rushing through him. He *had* been in solitary confinement for what seemed like half an eternity.

How long since he had been with a woman?

How long since he had been with a beautiful woman?

But then, he was making assumptions. Her beauty might make it impossible for him to get her alone. Would she be repulsed by the look of him? The High Priestess of Nimue had certainly increased the challenge, but he refused to be daunted.

Troy strode toward Drakina with purpose, as if there could be no doubt that she belonged with him. He halfway thought she would flinch, or turn aside, maybe run, but he'd underestimated this dragon princess.

Drakina surveyed him and smiled.

In fact, her eyes lit with fire, a sight that sent a thrill through him to his toes.

Maybe her demise could be delayed a little bit.

Drakina spotted her prey immediately, leaning against the bar, watching the door.

She had the odd sense that the Carrier had been waiting for her, that maybe there was a flicker of recognition in his eyes, but that made so little sense that she dismissed the notion.

The fact was that her destined mate was far uglier than she could have believed. She shuddered at the sight of him and her determination quailed.

The hologram had been flattering.

But then the Carrier stepped toward her with such confidence that she was surprised. He clearly believed that she should find him interesting, though he was the least attractive man in the bar, and he strode toward her with such verve and grace that Drakina *did* find him intriguing.

How often did she, a dragon shifter, meet a man who approached her with confidence? Was he fearless or a fool? Of course, the Carrier was unaware of her abilities, but she had to wonder whether the knowledge would have mattered. He strode toward her as if it were unthinkable that she should consider another.

Or as if he intended to ensure that she didn't.

Drakina liked that.

He moved like a warrior, all lithe grace and power. She liked that, too. Drakina watched him with rising anticipation, knowing that a man so in command of his body would be a memorable lover.

This mating might not be so bad.

The Carrier was taller than she was, at least in

this form, his hair dark and his eyes even darker. His shoulders were broad, and he was muscled in a most pleasing way. There was a blue mark on his flesh, a tattoo on his forearm, and she liked that it was a dragon. Kismet. She considered the merit of claiming him in the midst of this place, but recalled that Terrans preferred to practice such intimacy in private. As much as she wanted to seduce him quickly, she knew it would be smarter to let him set the pace.

For the moment.

The Carrier paused before her and she smelled the warmth of his skin, the heat of the ripe seed within him. She could feel the air heating between them and heard him catch his breath. His pulse had increased its pace and his eyes had brightened.

So, he did find her alluring.

Drakina smiled. Sexual awareness needed no other language to reveal itself than the body's reactions. She was warm herself, tingling a little, ready for him.

He halted before her and offered his hand. "Dance?" he invited, his voice a low rumble that made Drakina want to purr.

Dance. Of course. A mating ritual in so many cultures and societies. Drakina cast a glance at the other couples and knew she could sway as they did. In fact, she loved to dance, particularly with a masterful partner.

Was he one?

"Thank you." When she put her hand in his, the Carrier's fingers closed over hers in a proprietary gesture that she found most satisfactory. His hand was warm, his skin a little rough. He worked with his hands then, either a warrior or an artisan, both of which were admirable and noble occupations to Drakina's thinking.

She found her resistance to him melting.

And that was before he swung her onto the dance floor and turned her expertly. Her skirt flared, baring her legs above her knees, and she felt wanton, daring, unleashed. She recalled the sirens of the market and knew that she couldn't let her uncertainty show. She *was* bold, maybe even wanton. No one would ever know what she had done on Terra except gather the Seed. The other Terrans stepped back, making space on the dance floor for them, and Drakina surrendered to the pleasure of dancing.

They moved together as if they had danced this way a thousand times. All the while, his attention was fixed upon her, his gaze filled with admiration. His fingers brushed her hip, her shoulder, her waist, his attention unwavering. He said nothing, but there was no need for words. The air between them almost crackled with awareness, and the heat was enough to bring salt to Drakina's lip. She felt powerful and beautiful, alluring.

And aroused.

He made her look good, twisting her, dipping her, spinning her, his eyes lighting when she laughed with pleasure. The best warriors danced with such power and skill, and Drakina's desire for him grew.

She could hear his heartbeat and felt her own match its pace.

She could hear his breathing, and felt her own match its rhythm.

She was lost in his admiration, and felt the inevitability of their union become stronger. It would be fast and hard.

Maybe they would couple twice, just to be sure the Seed was planted.

The Carrier's lips curved just a little in an appreciative smile as he watched her, and Drakina couldn't look away from his mouth. There was something endearing about that smile, something that warmed her reaction considerably. He found her attractive. He was confident. His smile was sexy, perhaps because it was his best feature, perhaps because it seemed intimate, shared only with her. It seemed that all the rest of the occupants of the place disappeared.

There was only the Carrier and his alluring little smile.

She found herself studying his mouth, so fine and firm, so enticing. It was odd, because the hologram made it look as if he had an underbite, a most unattractive and bestial look, but there wasn't a thing wrong with his mouth. It was perfect, in fact. She couldn't wait to find out how he might kiss.

The music changed again, the fourth or fifth tune they'd danced, yet the Carrier showed no signs of tiring.

Much less of leaving the floor.

The other Terrans watched them, some applauding, yet Drakina wondered how she might hasten his mating ritual.

Subtlety wasn't one of her strengths, so she had no qualms about making her desires known.

Troy and Drakina danced. Fast and slow, close and far. He swung her and dipped her, he waltzed with her and he rhumba'd with her. She matched him step for step, never out of breath, never flagging. She seemed to anticipate his every move, and they could have always danced together. It was exhilarating—and exciting. Magical.

It made him remember what it was like to be in love.

Not that love had anything to do with this quest. No. He would do what had to be done, and he would survive.

Troy was simply charming her.

Winning her trust.

Although that sounded like an excuse even to himself.

The amazing thing was that he wasn't MindBending her. Not at all. Her reaction was genuine, and that astonished him. He wanted to savor it. He wanted to make this moment last.

It couldn't hurt to dance to one more song.

The blush in her cheek, the touch of her breasts, the weight of her hand in his, the throaty sound of her laughter all combined to convince Troy that Drakina was the most gorgeous woman he'd ever known. When the tune changed to a slow dance, Troy was glad. He wanted her close, pressed against him.

He placed his hand on the back of Drakina's waist and drew her near. Their bodies bumped and he realized how well they would fit together, the touch of her breasts and hips sending new fire through him. She watched him and her smile broadened, doubtless because she felt his erection.

Then she wrapped her arm around his waist and pulled him even closer, rolling her hips once against him in a clear demand.

And he'd expected a crown princess to be demure.

She looked up at him again and he was snared. She had the most remarkable green eyes. The irises seemed to glitter, as if made of faceted glass. She dropped her gaze to survey him, which made her look sultry.

Her coy smile sent fire through his blood.

"You are aroused," she murmured and he liked how low and lazy her voice was. Her words were melodic, almost as if she purred a song to him. She leaned into his embrace and touched her lips to the side of his neck. Troy could have sworn that the light kiss launched fireworks under his skin.

"I'm only human," he said, though that wasn't quite the truth.

She laughed. "I smell your excitement," she whispered and he closed his arms more tightly around her. "It is enticing for a woman to know that a man desires her."

It had been so long since he'd been with a woman—solitary confinement did have that drawback—and he'd forgotten how powerful a woman's touch could be.

"How could I not?" he murmured and her green eyes sparkled. "I've never danced with such a beautiful woman."

"Do you feel lucky then?"

"Of course." Troy held her a little tighter and she

arched her back, driving those breasts against him. He wondered for a moment who was being charmed. "What's your name?"

Drakina laughed a little, then he felt her tongue on his throat. "It doesn't matter," she whispered, her breath fanning his ear and making him shiver with anticipation. All he could think about was Drakina, her curves, her touch, her voice. Her fingers were in his hair, her hand firm against the back of his waist, her lips on his ear. "Tell me," she murmured. "How do you make love to a woman?"

They danced, turning tight circles on the floor, lost in each other.

"Slowly," he said, then swallowed. "Thoroughly." He bent and nuzzled her neck, kissing her beneath her ear. She gasped and rubbed herself against his chest. The feel of her was driving every thought from his mind.

Except one.

It occurred to Troy that seducing her would be a way to win her trust. To disarm her. To make her vulnerable.

He knew it was a rationalization. He couldn't have stepped away from her in this moment to save his life.

And wouldn't. Not yet.

"Never fast?" she whispered, mischief in her tone. She pulled back to look into his eyes and pouted, her expression playful. "I like when a man loses control," she admitted in a husky voice and Troy couldn't quite catch his breath. "I like when desire takes command." Drakina watched her hands as she spread her fingers flat and eased her palms over his chest. Her lips were parted, and Troy could only think about kissing her.

Slowly and thoroughly.

The second time, he'd take her fast and hard.

Drakina's right hand lingered over his heartbeat, her smile knowing as it raced. "I like when my lover can't hold back his desire," she confessed in a husky whisper. Her eyes shone at the possibility and Troy wanted to be that lover. "I like when he's driven to a frenzy." Her voice dropped lower. "I like when his passion is consuming." She gripped his shoulders then and stretched to her toes, locking those ruby red lips over his.

Her kiss was sweet and hot, honey and fire, temptation and seduction and more than he could bear. Troy's mind went white.

His heart thundered.

Then he caught her closer, lifting her in his arms so that she was on the tips of her toes. He slanted his mouth over hers and met the passion of her kiss. Drakina framed his head in her hands with a growl of satisfaction and he took a couple of steps backward as their kiss turned incendiary. She crushed him against the bar with her body, wrapped one leg around his and kissed him as if she'd suck him dry.

Troy found his own mind being bent.

Drakina's hands were in his hair and she held him captive to her kiss, but even better, she seemed to be unable to get enough of him. She used her tongue, her teeth, her lips, as if she would feast upon him. Maybe devour him whole. Troy couldn't think of a better way to go, much less a way to slow things down.

Then he jumped when the bartender tapped him on the shoulder.

Hard.

"Family place," the bartender chided. Troy blinked at him, not really understanding the words. He couldn't understand anything with Drakina's lush mouth grazing his throat. The bartender offered Troy a key.

His room key. Troy blinked and looked around, realizing that most of the other people in the bar were watching him and Drakina with both surprise and interest.

How could he have forgotten himself?

"Thanks. Yeah." Troy took the key and smiled at Drakina. Her eyes were dark, her intensity enough to make him consider the merits of hard and fast. "Maybe a little privacy?" he suggested.

Her smile broadened, and her expression seemed triumphant to him, as if she'd been planning their departure ever since she'd arrived.

But no, *he* was the MindBender.

She just liked it fast.

She wanted it now.

She was used to getting whatever she wanted.

In this moment, he didn't have any desire to refuse her.

Drakina brushed her lips over his, dismissing his thoughts. "If it's close," she murmured, running a proprietary hand down his chest. "I want you now," she whispered.

And then what? Troy had no doubt that he'd sleep, just a little, in the aftermath and might miss his chance to fulfill his quest. She might leave. Why was she even here? The gamblers must have arranged it somehow...

He had to think clearly. Being alone with Drakina was a good thing. Being intimate with Drakina was impossible to resist. But he'd have to slow things down. He'd have to MindBend her, slide his notions into her thoughts, and continue the seduction his way. Take control.

It was risky, to MindBend an amorous dragon shifter in the proverbial heat of the moment, but Troy wasn't the best MindBender in the galaxy for nothing.

Maybe he'd find something in her thoughts that would make it easy to assassinate her. Dragon shifters couldn't be innocent, after all. There was some reason that the gamblers wanted her dead.

When he looked into her eyes, so drowsy with desire, Troy had a feeling he'd need every argument he could find in order to win this bet.

The Carrier led Drakina to a chamber on the third floor of the hotel. It was a simple room, not very large, equipped with a bed and a large flat screen on one wall. Near the entrance were two doors, one that hid a closet and one that concealed a room for cleaning. At the far end of the chamber was a large glass window, which offered a view of the open expanse before the badlands. The room was on the back side of the hotel, and the window faced away from the town.

The acoustics were terrible and the insulation non-existent. She could hear the music almost as loudly as when they'd been near the band, and water flushed in a room down the hall. There was a distant clatter from the kitchen and the smell of fat frying. It made her stomach growl, but first things first.

Food was better *after* sex.

Slowly and thoroughly. Drakina had to rid his mind of that nonsense. Fast and hard. Against a wall. Consuming. Uninhibited. Passionate. Incendiary. That was the way she liked sex.

That was the way she'd have the Carrier.

As a bonus, she could return home sooner.

She'd just have to over-rule his reservations.

She knew he'd like it her way once he tried it. Warriors always did prefer a quick conquest.

They were barely inside the room when she flung him onto the bed. He fell to his back on the mattress and she landed atop him, locking her hands around his head and feasting on that gorgeous mouth again. He made a little growl of protest, but Drakina made sure he was too busy to say much more. His body revealed that he liked her technique. She slanted her mouth over his and kissed him, using her tongue and her teeth to make him moan aloud. His hands trailed up the backs of her thighs, which made her shiver, then slipped under the hem of her dress and gripped her buttocks.

She felt his heartbeat skip, then accelerate. She smelled the arousal within him and knew she was making progress in driving him toward her goal. She straddled him, pressing him down into the bed. She felt the size of him, the readiness of him, and this time, she was the one who growled. He pulled her closer in silent demand.

This would be a mating to remember. He was

huge and hard, which meant there was absolutely no cause for delay. Drakina slipped her hand between them and unfastened the front of his jeans. It was a complicated closure, to her thinking, with a button and some interlocking metal tracks, which seemed ill-advised for such a location. Again, she reasoned that there was no accounting for cultural differences. Maybe it was how they ensured slowly and thoroughly. Drakina sat up, tugged his pants over his hips and freed him.

She stared.

He was magnificent.

Perhaps *this* was why he was her destined mate.

Drakina caressed him with one hand and saw the first glimmer of the seed easing forth with her encouragement. Success was close! She rolled to one hip and tore off her own underwear, not bothering to remove anything else. She was slick and hot, ready for all he had to give. Troy tried to say something but she kissed him to silence. She moved to straddle him again and reached to coax his strength inside her.

She would take him in an inferno of passion. She would set his blood afire. She would show him how magnificent desire could be. Drakina was burning with need and ready to explode.

But the Carrier rolled her to her back in a smooth and powerful gesture that she could only admire for its grace and decisiveness. She smiled up at him, perfectly willing to be claimed in this posture, if only once. He lowered his weight between her thighs and she wrapped her legs around him, drawing him closer even as he bent to kiss her. His kiss was teasing and potent, and she could feel the hardness of him nudging against her.

She hooked one heel behind his tight butt to drive him home but he broke their kiss and evaded her. He trailed kisses along his jaw to her ear, a tingling path of fire, then nipped her earlobe. "Slowly and thoroughly," he whispered, as if it were a threat. Drakina had no chance to make sense of the words before he slid down the length of her.

He caressed her breasts with his hands, then opened the front fastening of her dress with his teeth. It felt so good, his strong rough hands on her skin, that she didn't stop him. He cast her a playful glance that almost made her giggle, then his mouth closed over her bare nipple.

He caught the peak between his teeth and flicked his tongue against it, making it harder, making her writhe with pleasure. She reveled in his touch and was glad that he showed no signs of relenting. She was gasping when he released the tight bud, and then he lavished the same attention on the other. Drakina thought she might explode. She reached for him, intending to pull him up and complete the union, but he caught her wrists in his hands and held them captive.

"Not so hasty, princess," he growled, his chest vibrating against her thighs.

Drakina was startled by his address, then wondered whether it was just a Terran endearment. He moved lower before she could ask, blew her skirt out of the way and bared her thighs to his view.

She was as wet as a harlot, to be sure. Drakina flushed crimson, but the Carrier simply lowered himself to grant her a most intimate kiss.

There?

She froze. She choked. She had never shared such an embrace but once he had begun, she didn't want him to stop.

It felt marvelous.

Her legs parted and she welcomed his tongue, his glorious mouth, and yes, even the graze of his teeth. What exquisite torment! This skill must be why he was her destined mate!

Drakina moaned and gripped his hands, twisting in satisfaction beneath his amorous assault. She had never felt so conflicted, so on fire, so desperate for more and so desirous of a moment lasting forever. She felt her heart pound harder, her breath catch, her passion grow. The Carrier was relentless, more expert a lover than any she'd taken before. Unlike other warriors, his focus was upon her pleasure instead of his own. And he understood her needs. He courted her reaction. He fed it and encouraged it, and teased her in ways that even she could not have named.

She felt his body respond to her arousal, which was most seductive. Their pleasure was yoked together, giving her a new and wondrous sense of communion.

Drakina felt the tide rise, higher and faster than it ever had before. Her need doubled and redoubled. She wanted him inside her, but he defied her will and remained where he was.

Tormenting her with that glorious mouth.

She could not restrain herself when he grazed her gently with his teeth. Drakina screamed as the torrent broke. She locked her legs around the Carrier and thrashed as pleasure coursed through her body. She shook and then she trembled.

When she fell back on the bed, spent, she glimpsed his triumphant smile.

Yet before she had recovered, she reached for him. She hauled him alongside her and straddled him again, needing to see him satisfied as well. He was harder and larger than he had been, but she teased him with her fingertips, caressing him and tormenting him in return. He moaned. He writhed against the bed, but Drakina held him down.

"We have tried your way," she whispered. "Now mine." And she lowered herself atop him, welcoming his strength inside her. She felt him tremble deep inside and knew he could not bear the exquisite torment long. His heart was racing. His breath came quickly. His hands gripped her waist and his gaze burned into hers.

Drakina was ready again, roused by his touch more than she might have believed possible. She gripped his wrists as he had seized hers, locked her mouth over his, and began to move. She swallowed his moan, felt victory near...

Then a strange dream unfurled in Drakina's mind.

She was dancing with the Carrier again, in a dark and private chamber. She saw his knowing smile and felt her heart respond. She saw his hand, sliding over her shoulder. Slowly. Very slowly. Warm when it reached her bare skin. His hand was tanned and calloused, the hand of a man who worked, and it contrasted with the silken smoothness of her own pale skin. He was gentle, though, so gentle, that his touch kindled

*a spark deep inside her. A coal glimmered to life. A blaze was
lit anew. He spun her in front of him as they moved in time to
the music, admiring her, barely touching her, knowing how
much she wanted him and letting her simmer.*

Making her burn hotter.

Drakina felt her movements slow as she was
seduced by the dream.

Slowly and thoroughly.

Her mouth went dry. How long could he endure?
Could she leave him without knowing for sure?

*Drakina felt the warmth of his fingertips feather over her
back, then his lips touch her skin so gently. A caress of a
thousand butterflies. His finger traced little circles lightly over
her flesh. Fingertips and lips working together to awaken every
bit of her skin. To undermine her resistance. It was a
seduction that made her ache for the next brush of his skin
against hers.*

*He lifted the weight of her hair, ran his fingers through it,
eased it over her shoulder, then his lips burned against her
nape. She heard herself gasp. She felt her nipples bead. She
arched her back and demanded more.*

She halted her movements and sat up. The
Carrier's eyes glittered as he watched her astride him.
She bared her breasts, displaying herself to him, then
rolled the nipples between her fingers and thumbs.
She cast her head back, teasing him, and felt the
power of his reaction.

"Slowly and thoroughly," he whispered and
moved within her with a deliberation that left her
yearning.

In her dream, he moved behind her and she swayed to the music, aware of his gaze upon her. He tugged down the fastener at the back of her dress, one tiny increment at a time. When it was loosed, he moved closer, his hands sliding beneath the garment, his arms around her, his hands cupping her breasts. Drakina heard herself moan as he rolled her nipples between finger and thumb, teasing them to peaks as he kissed the side of her neck. He was tormenting her, teasing her, making it last—and she was melting, powerless, snared by the spell he cast...

Drakina blinked as she realized the truth. This dream wasn't her own. It was *his*.

He had put his thoughts into her mind.

The Carrier was a MindBender!

What travesty was this?

CHAPTER TWO

D rakina roared with fury as she recoiled from the Carrier's embrace.

Not just a Terran but a MindBender! Rage rolled through her and she reacted with lightning speed. In a heartbeat, she had shifted shape, her back slamming against the plaster of the ceiling and making it crumble.

She would have abandoned him, if he had not been the Carrier of the Seed.

She still needed him, though that realization just made her more angry.

Drakina snatched up the Carrier and swung her tail to break the large window. She leapt through the gap, heard an alarm sound, and took flight.

How *dare* he try to manipulate her thoughts?

"Hey, wait a minute," he began and Drakina wasn't interested in any plea for mercy. She was a crown princess of Incendium! No one dared to meddle in the minds of her kind.

She could have left him behind. She could have fried him in place and he would have deserved no less.

But Drakina didn't just need the seed. She preferred vengeance to be slow and deliberate.

He would pay.

She flew beyond the boundaries of the town, her wings pounding hard in her fury. Once they were in the desert, she hurled the Carrier at the ground with force. She didn't care what he broke when he fell. His audacity demanded punishment of the highest order. She breathed a plume of flames after him.

He hit the ground, then curled into a ball and rolled away, propelled by the wind of her breath and the torrent of fire. Drakina bellowed and burned him some more, pursuing him with fire and fury.

She smelled his clothes incinerating. She smelled his skin burning. She smelled his hair singeing. Yet his mental fingers were still in her mind, probing, seeking her secrets.

Trying to learn her secrets and shape her will.

It was outrageous!

Impertinent.

Unacceptable.

No mere Terran should intrude in the mind of a royal Wyvern.

"*Get!*" Drakina roared, then took another breath. "*Out!*" The ground trembled at the volume of her cry. She spewed fire hotter and brighter than any she had breathed before. "*Of my mind!*"

The Carrier loosed his grip upon her thoughts immediately, and she wondered whether he'd forgotten what he was doing. Maybe he had been overwhelmed in the heat of the moment, so to speak. She stopped breathing fire, though she glared at him as she hovered in the air and watched him. He had come to a halt against a wall of rock.

He looked a little bit less confident. Shaken, but he deserved as much in Drakina's view. He lifted his head and looked around warily, watching her as he held up one hand in a universal gesture requesting clemency.

"Easy now," he said, with surprising bravery.

Drakina snarled, loosing an array of sparks. "I understand why my cousins devour their mates after they've served their purpose."

"There's no need to be hasty," he said, his tone soothing. "Let's talk it through."

There was something to be said for a man who didn't turn and run when faced with a larger and stronger adversary. Drakina felt her admiration return.

Still, she spoke sternly. "Out loud, MindBender."

"Right." He stood up and a part of her was relieved that he wasn't badly injured. His chest was mostly exposed, with shreds of his shirt hanging around his waist. He did offer an enticing view. His hair was a little shorter than it had been and his skin on the back of his shoulders was a little bit red. As if he'd been sunburned.

But there was a dignity in the way he stood, and she had to admit that she was almost as vexed by his mistake as by the interruption of a passionate interlude of considerable promise. For a moment there, Drakina had forgotten that she was seducing him for king and planet.

And then she realized something. Terrans didn't believe in dragons or shape shifters —yet the Carrier, a Terran, was unsurprised by the form she had just taken.

Drakina breathed a plume of fire at his feet, compelling him to dance backward. "Who are you really?" she demanded, her tone as imperious as it could be.

"My name is Troy." He offered that crooked smile, and Drakina was appalled that it softened her anger so much. "You've already figured out that I'm a MindBender." His gaze roved over her. "I do like smart women."

Drakina caught her breath, trying to fortify her resistance to him. It was fading fast. "You had no right..."

"No, I didn't." He sounded contrite. "I'm sorry."

Drakina wasn't quite prepared to forgive him—even if she was tempted by his appearance and that wretched smile. She sat back on her haunches, waiting. Her kind could be patient beyond most other species.

She would wait for a better apology, at least.

The Carrier eyed her for a moment, then walked toward her, proud even in his vulnerability. Not many men would willingly walk toward an angry dragon, especially after that dragon had just tried to fry them alive.

Was he brave or stupid?

Not stupid. Anything but stupid. Drakina had to bet on brave.

A warrior. Her heart clenched at what a fitting father he would make for their son.

"It was an act of desperation. I just wanted the whole thing to last a little longer," the Carrier said, that smile making it hard to hold such a desire against him. "It was so amazing."

"It was," she felt compelled to admit.

"*You* are amazing. I knew there was something different about you." He looked at her wings, her tail, her splendid scales, her trailing feathers and his admiration was clear. She fought the urge to preen and reminded herself that he should have been shocked by the sight of her. "You are *really* something."

"And how many other dragon shifters have you known, Terran?" she asked, her voice low with threat.

"None."

"Yet you were unsurprised by my abilities."

That smile broadened. "But you already know why, princess." His eyes shone with confidence and she knew the choice of endearment hadn't been an accident. "You caught me in your thoughts, but that was the *second* time I peeked."

If he had bent her mind without her detecting it, then he was highly skilled. Despite the insult, Drakina regarded the Carrier with new respect.

Was this the trait that he was to give to their son? A dragon shifter and MindBender might make a very potent crown prince.

And a successful king.

"In fact, that gives us something in common," he continued easily. "We both have secrets." He heaved a sigh. "Imagine finding the one person you can trust who knows your secret. That's where we are."

She supposed it might be an appealing notion for some, but everyone in her life knew what she was.

"We have desire in common," Drakina said flatly.

"That is enough for this encounter, or it might have been if you had kept your thoughts to yourself."

"I think we should talk about this," he continued, his manner so assured that he might have believed the discussion inevitable. "Why can't there be more than one encounter? What if there's a future for us?"

Drakina laughed. She couldn't help it.

The Carrier didn't look insulted. No, he gave her a look that was so stubborn that if he had been more handsome, she might have been reminded of the sons of royal blood of her acquaintance. "You want me," he said, reminding her of the truth. "I want you. Let's talk first."

It was a telling reminder. Drakina *needed* him, and his seed.

"You will not surrender to me without a discussion first?"

"Nope." He grinned, confident that she would cede to him.

His cockiness was entirely undeserved. Drakina knew she could seduce him, even against his own will, because the attraction between them was strong.

Still, it might be a bad portent for a crown prince to be conceived against the Carrier's will.

And a conversation was a comparatively small concession.

It wouldn't take much time.

She might convince him to surrender in a blaze of passion yet.

"Stay out of my mind," Drakina stipulated. "Because next time, I won't stop."

"Promise not to roast me if I do stay out of your mind," the Carrier countered and offered his hand.

He was so intrepid that she admired him even more.

His was a charming Terran gesture, although Drakina hadn't recognized its appeal when she'd read about it in her research. His move, in silence, conveyed the notion of compromise, a concept not particularly dear to Drakina but which might be useful in pursuit of her quest. On the other hand, her word was her bond, and if she pledged this to him, she would keep that vow at any cost.

She considered his hand for only a moment before she shifted shape, assuming her woman form again. Her dress was still unfastened at the front but she couldn't have cared less. She felt the leap of Troy's pulse at the glimpse of her breasts, though, and knew he was very aware of her physically.

That could only help in achieving her goal.

In fact, their conversation might be very short. She chose to leave her dress open to aid in that and stepped closer to put her hand in his. "I am Drakina." She put her hand in his and they shook hands. She liked the feel of his warm fingers gripping hers.

"How do you do that?" he asked with real curiosity.

"Do what?" She couldn't explain to him how she shifted shape. It was an innate power, but one that required considerable training to master effectively.

"Be naked as a dragon, then still have your dress in human form."

"Initiate's secret," Drakina said mysteriously, having no intention of giving him any power over her. Her gaze trailed to his lips and she hoped they might seal the bargain with a kiss. That was another

Terran tradition, and a very appealing one.

The Carrier smiled as if he knew her inclination and began to lean closer.

Drakina glared at him and he lifted his hand in surrender.

"It was in your eyes," he protested. "I didn't need to look in your mind."

So, he was perceptive. Drakina considered herself warned. His kiss this time was fleeting, a tease and maybe a promise.

Or maybe a way to keep his desire reined in.

He quickly released her hand and stepped back, and she saw the evidence that he was not unmoved by their quick embrace. He pushed one hand through his hair. "Look, there's an all-night diner in town. How about something to eat?"

It appeared that he didn't need to be a MindBender to anticipate her needs.

He kept talking, as if to convince her. "I can go back to the room and get your panties as well as a new shirt, then meet you downstairs."

"You cannot escape me," she reminded him with quiet force. "I trailed you across the cosmos by scent."

"Kismet?" he asked, his tone teasing.

"Of course." Drakina touched the tattoo on his forearm.

He smiled at her so that her heart leapt. His eyes twinkled in a way that made them look less small and beady. "What makes you think I want to get away, princess?" His confidence was enticing indeed, and Drakina found herself smiling back at him.

Then she watched avidly as he strode back to the

hotel, purpose in his every move.

Yes, her Carrier was a very tasty specimen, even if he was a MindBender. Drakina found herself looking forward to both the fortification of food and the consummation of their fated partnership.

She might even regret leaving him behind.

It was more than a shirt Troy needed. He had to be sure that no one had noticed Drakina's spectacular departure from the hotel, or there'd be more questions than either of them could answer.

To his relief, there was only a pair of kids from the kitchen standing in the alley behind the hotel, along with a police officer, amidst the broken glass of the window. He didn't have time to think of a very good story—he walked in his sleep, broke through the window, stumbled down the fire escape and then ran—but his MindBending abilities came to the rescue. Only one kid had seen Drakina in dragon form and it was pretty easy to convince him that he'd been imagining things. There were no dragons, after all. Troy said he'd pay for the window, which satisfied the cop, then he saw Drakina strolling into view.

All three of his companions turned to stare.

And no wonder. She was gorgeous. Confident. Now he saw the dragon in every move she made. It was more than that long flaming red hair and those glittering green eyes. That sinuous walk. Never mind the way she looked over people, as if assessing how tasty they might be. She looked like she had a passion for pleasure and sensation.

As if she'd be insatiable.

He was glad to see that she'd refastened her dress. Even covered, her figure could stop traffic. And she was mating with him. Troy felt a surge of pride, then hurried up to the room as promised. He took a couple of minutes to shave as well as change his shirt, wanting to look his best.

Such as it was.

Troy knew what he had to do, but the way he figured it, he still had one day to do it.

When was he going to have another chance to be with a dragon shifter princess? He was going make these few hours count.

Even so, he felt a strange uneasiness. What did Drakina mean when she said that she had tracked him across the cosmos by scent? Why would she do that? How would she even know his scent?

His gut clenched. What else hadn't the gamblers told him?

Once they were seated in the diner, Drakina avidly surveyed the occupants and the menu. Troy had explained the use of menus to her, when she would have simply given a command to the chef. She perused it with shining eyes and quickly made a decision.

She could probably smell the exact inventory of food in the place.

Troy watched her in awe and wonder. A dragon princess. With him! It was easy to remember all his childhood fantasies, and he certainly wasn't disappointed in the reality.

Drakina cast him a smile that seemed conspiratorial when the food came and Troy couldn't help but smile in return. She devoured her two eggs over easy with bacon, toast, and hash browns. He was fascinated by how fastidiously she ate. Her manners were perfect, but she ate very quickly, and there wasn't a molecule left when she was done.

She looked disappointed when her plate was clean and eyed his bacon with such obvious interest that he almost laughed.

Troy pulled his own plate closer, protective of it because he was starving. She smiled and he saw the dragon in that expression, too.

"So, where are you from?" he asked, for lack of a better opening.

"Why should I tell you more than you know?"

"Because I want to learn more about you." He realized that it was true. He wasn't just trying to charm her. He really wanted to know. "I'm curious."

"A perilous inclination, Carrier."

Carrier? Carrier of what? "Maybe," Troy replied with a chuckle, wanting to keep the conversation on an even keel. It was tempting to peek into her mind, but he didn't think he'd survive to tell the tale the second time. He had to find out about her the old-fashioned way. "But what's the harm in it? It might feel good to confide in someone."

"I have attendants at home."

"Friends?"

"Sisters."

"Not quite the same."

"No." Her eyes narrowed as she considered him and his proposition. "Is this part of slow and thorough?"

"You could say that."

"The confession must be reciprocal."

"Three questions each?" he suggested and she thought about it for only for a moment before nodding.

"And you have asked one already. I am from the Kingdom of Incendium."

"Which is the twin planet of Regalia," he said before he thought twice.

Her eyes lit with surprise. "You were efficient in your MindBend."

Troy had to think fast to cover his mistake. "Call it a habit. Get in, get what you need and get out."

"Like a thief."

"More like a spy."

She arched a brow, unconvinced.

"So, you're from Incendium." He had to steer a careful course between revealing what he knew and asking her enough to win her confidence. "And you're here because...?"

"Because of you," she said immediately and his heart skipped despite her matter-of-fact tone. "You are the Carrier and I will conceive with your Seed. It has been foretold." She confided this last detail as if that explained everything.

Troy supposed that it did, but he was shocked all the same. "Maybe I don't want to." He definitely didn't want to conceive a child with Drakina then kill her.

She fixed a look on him that could have cut glass and he knew he had to give her some explanation.

"Maybe I'm shy."

She chuckled at that.

"Maybe I don't want kids."

She dismissed this with a gesture. "It will cost you nothing to surrender the Seed. Your role then will be complete."

She could only think that because she didn't know what he was supposed to do. "Maybe I'm not certain I'll survive it."

Drakina leaned across the table, holding his gaze. "The son I conceive will be the crown prince and the hope of our world. I'm not leaving without the Seed." Her smile was chilly. "No matter what I have to do to claim it."

Troy was well aware in that moment that they were both predators. It was a timely reminder.

He was careful to not use a question for his response. He'd used up two already. "Because it's been foretold. I don't believe that anyone knows what's going to happen in the future."

"Nor do I." Drakina's voice dropped to a confidential tone. "I don't care much about destiny. I'm the oldest of the royal princesses and my father has always had plans for me to perpetuate his dynasty. If bearing this one son means he lets me make my own choices, I'll do it."

"The oldest," Troy mused, feeling a familiar yearning. "I have no brothers or sisters."

"And kin?"

He liked that she'd asked a question about him. "My mom died when I was a teenager."

"And your father?"

"Careful, princess, that's two," he teased and she flushed. "He died a bit later, after I was eighteen. I was alone then on the farm." It was easy to recall how confined he'd felt in those days. How lonely.

"Solitude," Drakina said, exhaling slowly. "It sounds like paradise. I'm envious of you, Carrier."

He looked up to find her watching him with that assessing smile, the dragon smile that made his heart leap. The fact was that he didn't think much of solitude. Being alone was what had allowed the pirates of Manganus Five to capture him. Being alone in the penal colony of Xanto had driven him crazy enough to accept this insane, long-shot of a deal.

At least it had brought him to Drakina. She was unlike anyone he'd ever known.

She reminded him of what it was to be alive, instead of just existing.

He was caught. He couldn't complete the mission without having her once, yet now that he'd met her, he didn't want to complete it at all.

Was there another way out?

Troy's gaze dropped to Drakina's lips and she ran the tip of her tongue across the top one, tantalizing him with the reminder of her kiss. He swallowed and averted his gaze, knowing he had to delay the seduction as long as possible. She might leave as soon as it was done.

"I want that," she murmured and his heart jumped. To his surprise, she reached out to indicate his last piece of bacon.

"Forget it," he retorted. "It's the best part of breakfast. I always save it to the last." He didn't eat it though, because he might be able to negotiate with it.

"You eat this often? Daily?"

"Not always now, but we ate it all the time when I was a kid."

"What do you call it?" She lifted a finger in warning. "That doesn't count as my third question, Carrier. It is a linguistic enquiry, not a question about you."

He smiled. "Bacon."

"And you ate it often because it is a typical choice of sustenance?"

"My parents' farm was for raising pigs and boars. There was always a lot of pork."

Drakina repeated the words several times. "It reminds me of verran." Her expression turned bleak.

"Is that a problem?" Her gaze flicked to his and he echoed her gesture. "Not my third question."

She laughed. "Not in itself. The taste just provokes memories."

"Like what?"

She gave him an intent look, even as she smiled. "You are a curious Terran. Don't you know that it's risky to provoke my kind?"

Troy arched a brow. "Maybe I like to live dangerously."

"It is the mark of a warrior to be bold in the face of peril," she said softly and her eyes glowed with promise.

Their gazes held for an electric moment and Troy felt the heat rising inside him. If she leaned across the table and touched him, even if her fingers landed on his hand, he'd be lost all over again...

But Drakina shook her head and, to Troy's surprise, she answered his question. Her tone was dreamy. "When I was a child, we went to Sylvawyld, a heavily forested small moon in our system, during the harvest season. My father hunted verran there, for they are plentiful and sufficiently fierce to challenge him. We dined often on their meat and the servants smoked the remainder to take home afterward."

"Your father is a good hunter, then?"

"He is a king," she said with some hauteur. "It is his privilege and his responsibility." Her gaze dropped to the bacon and Troy wondered whether he could eat it and live to tell about it.

Then she licked her lips slowly. "I would do almost anything to taste verran again."

There was an enticing proposition. "Anything?" Troy pushed the plate across the table. Her eyes glittered, then she took the bacon and devoured it.

Delicately and quickly.

"It is almost the same," she said, scanning the empty plates with obvious regret.

"You'll be able to have some more when you get back to Incendium."

Drakina shook her head. "The verran were hunted to extinction by the Regalians half a lifetime ago."

"Who?"

"Regalia is the other planet and kingdom in Incendium's solar system. The Regalians live there."

"Are they shifters too?"

"No. Maybe that explains *everything*." She winced.

Troy left that alone, since he wasn't a shifter either. "Why would they hunt the verran to extinction?"

Drakina's look was pitying. "Because they are too stupid to consider the future."

"Probably better you didn't marry one, then." He

meant to tease her, but she snorted.

"Where is it written that I did not?"

"You're married?" Troy wondered then if there was more behind this bet he had been compelled to participate in.

"Not quite. I was supposed to marry, but there was a complication." She gave him an intent look. "I am too famished, Carrier, to confide more of this tale."

"Is that an offer I can't refuse?"

"Perhaps one you should not." Her smile was seductive, though.

"Do you want more breakfast?"

"Another of the same," she admitted, then glanced over the diner. "But these Terrans are temperate in their appetites, and I don't want to attract attention."

It was too late for that, but Troy wasn't going to tell her as much. She was too striking to avoid attention.

"I can fix it," he offered.

Drakina smiled, understanding immediately. "Your gift can be used for such a feat?"

He nodded.

"Ah, so there is some merit in this rare skill." She sat back like a queen. "Then, please do, MindBender."

The Carrier enchanted the waitress easily.

She was small and pale for a Terran, and Drakina could smell that she hated her job. She couldn't imagine why the Terran did nothing to change her situation. The waitress was not a slave, but she was

as resentful as one. Drakina had noticed the waitress'
interest in the Carrier when they entered the diner,
and now the Carrier used her interest against her.

It was a clever tactic.

He turned that smile upon the small Terran when
she came back to fill his coffee cup. Drakina hadn't
touched hers, because she didn't like the beverage.

"Thanks so much," the Carrier said, his tone as
warm as his smile.

The waitress looked at him, parted her lips to say
something, then Drakina saw that she was snared.
The Carrier held her gaze and she could almost feel
the power of his influence. In a way, it was a relief to
know that she wasn't the only one fascinated by his
smile.

In another, it disappointed her to have anything
in common with this waitress, who disliked her job
and did nothing about it. Drakina could not abide
such passivity.

Even in a stranger.

"Would you like anything to eat?" the waitress
asked, her voice sounding dreamy.

"I'm good with coffee," the Carrier said. "But the
lady wants breakfast." He listed the same meal she
had just consumed and the waitress nodded. "Extra
bacon," he added.

"Absolutely." The waitress cleared away the dirty
plates, apparently without noticing the inconsistency
in what she did, then soon returned with a new meal.
She served it as if she hadn't done the exact same
thing just moments before.

Drakina inhaled the scent of it with pleasure.
This bacon was powerfully nostalgic for her,

reminding her of marvelous times at hunt. She ate the first piece with pleasure, knowing that the Carrier watched her with some pride in what he had done.

He deserved praise.

He deserved a reward.

"It is the way of my kind to put more emphasis on deeds than words," she began. "You have done this for me, so in thanks, I will do what you desire of me." Drakina was sure he would ask for slow sex, but the Carrier surprised her.

"Three wishes?" he asked, a teasing glint in his eye.

Drakina smiled. "Three wishes," she agreed.

"First, some more conversation," he stipulated. "Then make a little trip with me." Drakina was intrigued. His smile widened. "You can guess the third wish."

"Because it is also mine?" she replied and he laughed. Ah, he looked younger and more carefree when he laughed and the sound was most alluring. "Still we will dispute the speed of the union."

"Maybe so," he admitted and stole a piece of her toasted bread. He was welcome to it. "Tell me about Incendium," he invited. "I've heard only statistics. Tell me why you love it."

"You're MindBending in a different way," she accused and he grinned. He was not so foul to look upon as she had first thought. In fact, he grew more appealing with every moment she spent in his company. It was his nature that beguiled her and blinded her to his physical appearance.

The fact was that Drakina was enjoying his company.

"I have to learn about you the way everyone else does," Troy said. "Come on, tell me."

"Incendium is one of a pair of planets orbiting the same sun. Regalia is the other. My kind rules Incendium, while a species who cannot shift shape rules Regalia. They look much like Terrans."

"And Incendium is filled with shifters?"

"No. We intermarry with those who do not shift. On Incendium, both shifters and those who do not shift live in communities together, the tale being that the strengths of each kind balance the weaknesses of the other. Destined mates are usually of the other species."

"Does everyone have a destined mate, or just the royal family."

She considered this with a frown. "I expect that everyone does, but may not know of it. The best astrologers labor in my father's court, and cast horoscopes only for the royal family."

"And on Regalia?"

Her lips tightened. "They are said to prefer sorcery over science."

"But the two planets have peaceful relations?"

"Notoriously not, not for a long time. But my grandfather brokered a treaty with the Regalians, and it has been honored all this time."

"Even after they hunted the verran to extinction."

"Even then, though matters were precarious for a century or two." It was easy to guess the reason for his confusion. "It would have been comparable to three hundred years ago in Terran time." The Carrier blinked and Drakina anticipated his next question.

She pulled her interpretor from the pocket in her dress that disguised it and tapped a query. "I was born the Terran equivalent of four hundred and fifteen years ago. We are considered children for eighty-one Terran years." She smiled. "Ha! It is also a magic number on Terra. Nine times nine. The most potent magical number of all." She put the computer away and returned to the matter at talon. "And so, we have been more or less at peace with the Regalians these five hundred years."

"Because you found harmony?"

"More recently, because we discovered that we face a common threat. This is what enabled us to move beyond the loss of the verran. Each rotation of our system brings both planets closer to our sun. It is forecast by both the astrologers and the sorcerors that soon both planets will fall into the fiery heat of the sun and be destroyed."

"How is any son you bear supposed to prevent that?"

Drakina shrugged. "I don't know." She put down her fork, deciding to be honest. "I don't actually believe it can be done."

"The kingdoms could unite and colonize."

"And each surrender some authority to the other? You know little of dragons, Carrier, and less of kings. They will each die in their respective kingdoms. We are comparatively isolated in the galaxy and transport is expensive. It may not even be possible to build enough transport vessels for the entirety of both populations. The kings must work together for a solution."

"But if you don't believe in the prophecy, why

are you here?"

"Because my father does believe and because I am prepared to fulfill his desire in exchange for mine."

The Carrier arched a brow.

"Freedom," she said. "The right to choose."

"What would you choose to do instead of being a crown princess?"

"Do not be impertinent, Carrier," Drakina chided. "The royal whim is not yours to know." He fell silent, though there was a predictable mutiny in his eyes. At least he kept his mind to himself. She finished her meal and pushed the plate aside, wishing there had been more bacon.

She looked up to find his eyes twinkling. How had she ever thought them small and beady?

"Again?" he murmured.

Drakina smiled. "You read it in my eyes."

"You're an open book, princess."

She couldn't help but chuckle. "You desire only more of my truth."

The Carrier leaned forward, an alluring intensity in his manner. "I *like* pleasing you," he whispered, his words sending a thrill through her. "Slowly and thoroughly." Their gazes clung over the table and Drakina's mouth went dry. She let him see the truth of what she wanted to do to him, in her eyes. The Carrier swallowed and moved restlessly on the opposite bench, showing a most enticing impatience.

She would convince him of the merit of fast sex before their ways parted.

"Again," she agreed. "And possibly once more after that. I believe I will be needing my strength."

She smiled at him. "It might be wise to fortify yourself as well, Carrier."

CHAPTER THREE

S o, you're the oldest?" Troy prompted when Drakina was tucking into her third breakfast. He was wondering how to bring the conversation back to her marriage. What had happened to the lucky guy? He liked that she confided in him, but then she was a dragon shifter. She wasn't going to lose many fights. "Of how many?"

"There are twelve princesses in the royal brood of Incendium."

"All dragon shifters?"

She nodded, as if this was self-evident.

"But if you're the oldest princess, shouldn't you be making a dynastic match?"

Drakina's smile was quick. "My father tried that." He guessed his curiosity was obvious because she set down her fork. "Once upon a time," she began and he almost laughed. "The Queen of Regalia bore twelve sons. The King of Incendium, my own father, sired twelve daughters." Her expression turned rueful. "If you know anything at all of kings and their desire to organize the lives of those beneath their hand—or claw, as the case might be—you can guess what happened."

"They wanted to match their daughters and sons in marriage."

"So predictable." Drakina surveyed the remainder of her meal and reached—predictably—for the bacon. "And so I was to be the first because I was the oldest. So was he. The betrothal was announced, and the preparations were made. The heralds were dispatched and the festivities arranged."

"What was he like?"

She gave him a chilling glance. "Sinewy. It must have been all that jousting."

Sinewy?

Troy stared at her as she calmly ate another piece of bacon.

She nodded, as if in recollection. "With a definite and lingering aftertaste." She shuddered. "I'd so hoped he'd be sweet."

"You *ate* him?"

"I had just cause." Her manner was prickly. "The tribunal court agreed."

"I'm skeptical of that." This put a different slant on being the Carrier of the Seed. She had mentioned that her cousins eliminated their mates once they had fulfilled their usefulness. Would killing Drakina be an act of self-defense?

Drakina granted him a simmering glance, then leaned forward, stabbing one finger into the table as she argued her own case. Troy felt the force of her anger, but he knew it would be foolish to retreat. He might end up looking like lunch.

She breathed the words so low that the table

vibrated. "He. Stood. Me. Up."

"Not at the altar."

Drakina returned to her meal and ate with savage haste, her eyes flashing. "*Of course*, at the altar. In my father's palace. With dignitaries from every ally in attendance. Do you know what that wedding cost my father? What it cost his kingdom? And that foul excuse for a prince didn't even have the courage to break off the engagement in person. He sent a *clerk*." She sneered and Troy was sure he saw sparks. "Canto was no warrior."

"He was unworthy of you."

"Exactly." She shoved the plate away with such force that it clattered against the wall at the end of the booth. There was even a piece of bacon on it still. She glared at Troy and he thought she might shift shape on the spot.

"I was mortified," she said, her words thrumming. "My father was furious. My mother was a wreck." She straightened, seeming to notice that the waitress and the cook were looking. She did a creditable job of composing herself before she continued. "So, I did the only reasonable thing. I left immediately to ensure justice. I shifted shape right then and there. I left the festivities in a cold, lethal rage, and hunted Canto to the ground. Just as he deserved."

It said something about her world that this reaction could be considered the only reasonable thing to do. Troy could just imagine her shifting shape, right in front of the company, then taking flight. She'd probably breathed a bit of fire as she'd flown around the building.

"My father *was* a bit vexed about the hole in the roof, but he understood my impulse. I think he might have let it pass if I hadn't found Canto so quickly and things hadn't been resolved so...absolutely." She lifted her hands. "He could not even *hide* well!"

"You might have let him live?"

She grimaced. "I *might* have been more temperate if there had been time for my temper to cool, but as it was, that was out of the question."

Troy thought it was a good idea to learn as much as possible about escaping her wrath, even though he didn't intend things to get to that. "Why was it out of the question?"

Drakina shook her head. "He liked a particular perfume and wore it often. He thought it was alluring." Her expression revealed that she didn't agree. "I believe the scent is known here, as well." She frowned and pulled out that small computer again. It was a kind he'd seen many times since he'd left Earth. It was so thin that it was essentially a film, and could be folded or adhered to skin, hidden in a tiny pocket like the one in Drakina's dress, yet had an astonishing computing power. Troy was belatedly impressed by her command of Terran English. She hadn't used the interpreter much at all.

She must have studied in preparation for the trip.

She laughed then and put the interpreter away. "A similar Terran perfume is called myrrh. But the ancient Egyptians used it for the embalming of corpses. I think I should have liked these Egyptians."

"They're long gone."

"So I see." She seized the final piece of bacon.

"Well, it led to *his* funeral, because I could have followed that trail of scent anywhere."

"What scent do you find alluring in a man?" Troy wanted to know and thought it would be a good idea to calm her temper.

Drakina's eyes sparkled immediately, then her voice dropped low. "His own. I like the musk of warm skin. It reveals desire and hints at pleasure." She leaned over the table and held his gaze as she inhaled slowly. "Your scent is good, Carrier," she whispered. "Man not meat. Warrior, not courtier."

That was good to know. "I'll guess there were repercussions from you hunting down the groom."

"A diplomatic incident, as they say, and my father's wrath to be faced. In the end, it was only the dire situation of our two planets that drew Regalia and Incendium into reluctant alliance again. At least, there is no question of my securing the bond."

"One of your sisters will have to do it?"

"Gemma is betrothed to Urbanus, the new crown prince, and I wish her luck. He's probably even less toothsome than his brother."

Urbanus? Troy's thoughts flew as he realized that the bet that had sent him on this mission wasn't a coincidence at all. There couldn't be two men named Urbanus, both the crown prince of Regalia, and both with a prince's conviction that his will should be done. Troy had hated the gambler on sight.

If his brother Canto had been anything like him, he would have been glad to see Drakina devour him.

But it explained why Urbanus wanted Drakina dead.

And wanted her assassinated badly enough to

make a wager on Xanto.

Troy looked around, feeling a strange lack of interest in fulfilling his mission, the one that was his only chance to survive. Was he losing his mind?

Or did he and the dragon princess have something unexpected in common, in that they had both been unjustly condemned?

Drakina cleared her throat delicately. "Strangely enough, the festivities have been delayed repeatedly."

"Maybe she shares your view."

"The astrologers keep saying the time is not right. I have wondered whether she is bribing them. Gemma tends to achieve her goals more quietly than I." Drakina considered Troy with a smile. "So, you see, I have been ill-fated in courtship and will only be pragmatic in future. I come here with one purpose. I want your Seed. Let us come to terms, Carrier. Incendium falls ever closer to the sun."

Troy had to prolong their discussion. "Don't you think that what I want matters? Just a little?"

She was clearly startled by the notion. "Why should I? I am a royal Wyvern. I am doing my duty in conceiving a son for the good of the realm."

"But you need my help to do that."

Drakina was both intrigued and surprised. "What *do* you want, Carrier?"

"That would be your third question," he warned.

"And it is a good one. I accept that it is my last query of you."

Troy didn't know what he was going to say until the words fell out of his mouth. "I don't want to be alone anymore, princess." Once he had said it, he knew it was true.

Even better, he knew he had to find another solution.

Somehow, he had to have Drakina *and* win the bet to survive.

Drakina's gaze brightened with curiosity. "Indeed?"

"I'm thinking that no matter what lies ahead for you and me, I'm going to want to see my son. Repeatedly. Maybe constantly. There will be no seed from me unless we come to an agreement on that."

Her eyes narrowed but her tone stayed level. "Terrans are not welcome in Incendium."

"You and I could stay here."

Drakina inhaled sharply and cast a glance of disgust about herself. "It's so primitive! You cannot mean to insist upon such a condition!"

Troy knew in that moment how he might change her mind. "I like it. It's home. You might come to like it too."

She arched a brow.

He smiled at her undaunted. "And the seed is mine to give or not."

Drakina's lips tightened but Troy didn't blink. Then she leaned across the table and dropped her voice low. Her fingertip landed on the back of his hand, then trailed upward. "I could seduce you into complying," she murmured and Troy knew she had a good chance of succeeding.

He drew his hand back, although he didn't want to. "You could," he admitted. "But it would hurt my feelings to be used like that, and you've already given your word that you won't injure me." It was a long shot and a technicality.

But it worked.

Drakina inhaled sharply, sat back, and glared at him. She drummed her fingers on the table. "Another sinewy one," she muttered. "Just my luck."

Troy smiled, just a little, and a flame lit in her eyes.

"Convince me of the merit of this place, Carrier. There must be some reason you are fond of it."

That was exactly what Troy had hoped she would say.

And he hadn't used his MindBending skills at all. He felt encouraged.

"That's why we're going on a little trip, princess. Wish number two." He surveyed the empty dishes. "Think you can last a couple of hours without a meal?"

"My curiosity is awakened. Where are we going?"

The strange thing was that the more her mate challenged her, the less unattractive Drakina found him to be. His intelligence shone in his eyes, along with his determination and his desire. His body was muscled and very alluring, his embrace both tender and tough. She liked that she could provoke his reaction with her touch. She liked that he talked to her. She liked best of all that he provoked her, both with words and deeds, and was unafraid of her.

He was such a warrior that she began to think that he was worthy of her.

After so many exchanges with the Regalian crown princes—who were supposedly so rugged and fearless but simpered and shook like butterflies in the presence of a Wyvern princess—his attitude was a relief.

It was also intriguing. He believed she would keep her word. Of course, Drakina *would* keep her word, but mortals who made tasty snacks for dragons were usually far less trusting.

He wasn't MindBending. Now that she was paying attention, she knew it. She had only to hear the sound of an intruder once to be alert to it forevermore.

Troy. She let herself think his name, then reminded herself not to get soft.

What gave him this confidence?

What had made him so resolute?

Drakina reminded herself the egg within her was ripe, and that it should be fertilized soon to avoid the potential for undesirable mutation. If her son was to save Incendium, he had to be perfect and whole. She had to have the Carrier's Seed soon.

Now.

As soon as his second wish was fulfilled.

He led her out of the diner and to an establishment across the street. The door was locked and he tapped on the glass. A woman appeared in the shadows of the darkened store and unlocked the door.

"Not open for another hour," she said.

"Could you make an exception?" the Carrier asked, and Drakina couldn't be sure whether he was MindBending or just using his natural charm. He seemed to have a lot of that. "We're in a bit of a hurry."

The woman pursed her lips. "Suppose it's foolish to turn down any business, now that the festival's over and done."

"The lady needs jeans and a jacket," the Carrier said. "Boots, too. We'll be riding my Harley."

The woman's face lit with an understanding Drakina did not share. She welcomed them into the shop and hastened to one side, almost dancing between the racks of garments and Drakina. "Try these first," she said, holding up a garment that would sheath her legs. "Our most popular line."

Drakina smiled at the Carrier in gratitude.

Within moments, she was more modestly clothed, the dress and sandals packed in a bag. When she came out of the small chamber in the jeans, the Carrier caught his breath in a most satisfactory way.

"Fit you like a second skin," the woman said.

Drakina found pleasure in the gleam of the Carrier's eyes.

By the time they left, she had a shirt and a jacket, a pair of gloves and boots. The Carrier led her to the back of the hotel, where a two-wheeled chariot awaited. He donned a helmet, handing a second one to her, then sat astride the bike. He started the engine, which had a very pleasing roar. Drakina climbed onto the vehicle behind him, liking that she could wrap her legs around him.

She caressed the tight curve of his butt and he cast her a look. If he was trying to look stern, the twinkle of his eyes undermined the effect.

"This is a Harley," she said, savoring its sound.

"This is *my* Harley," he corrected, then turned out of the lot. As soon as they were on the open road outside of town, he accelerated. The motor thrummed in a most satisfying way. The land raced past them. Drakina leaned against him, loving how vital and alert he was.

"It's almost as good as flying!" she shouted at him.

"That's what I always thought, princess."

It was too hard to talk so Drakina just enjoyed. She held tightly to her mate, feeling his muscles flex beneath her hands. They leaned into the curves together, and she reveled in the steady beat of his heart. She saw a mountain rise before them, way out in the distance, and believed there were trees upon it. It could have been Sylvawyld, except for the ribbon of road, for there were few other vehicles and they saw no people. The sky was clear overhead and their sun shone hot.

They could have been alone in Troy's world, just the two of them with no duties or obligations. Drakina found that a strangely alluring prospect.

And that was before she saw the corner of Terra he loved best.

It had been a long time.

But things hadn't really changed at the farm.

The drive still wound in from the highway, and the house and barn were still hidden behind the trees. The sight of the house still took his breath away, though the barn looked in need of some repair. The yard was empty, of course, and when he turned off the bike, the familiar silence pressed against his ears. Troy could hear a distant car and then the wind.

Drakina lifted her helmet off and surveyed the farm with obvious approval. "Verran," she whispered.

"Not any more. No one has farmed here for a decade."

She gave him a knowing look. "Are you sure, Carrier?"

He paused on the way to the front door, considering her. Could there be any livestock that survived? If there was, it would be the boars. They were half-wild anyway. "Are you kidding me?"

"I smell them." Her eyes narrowed and she inhaled again. She nodded.

"My dad had a sounder of boars."

Drakina frowned in confusion.

"It's what they call a small herd of boar," Troy explained. "The sows stay together in a sounder and raise the young. The males are solitary." He knew suddenly how he could explain the mating cycle to her. "It's a matriarchal society. The males return to the sounder only to share their seed, though they compete against each other for that privilege."

"So the strongest one sires the young." Drakina nodded approval of that. "My cousins have done this with their mates. The selection of the mate is a popular sport on their planet."

Those would be the cousins who ate their mates once the deed was done. Troy didn't want to encourage any of those ideas.

Drakina stood with the hands on her hips, sniffing as if she sampled the wind. "I smell perhaps five sows together, several with young—" She looked at him, a question in her eyes.

"Squeakers," he provided and she smiled.

"Do they squeak?"

"They do. They're really cute, actually."

Her smile was wistful. "I have never seen young verran. We always hunted in the season when the young had grown to size."

"That's responsible."

She nodded. "A herd must be managed well to ensure that it thrives. My father had three gamekeepers monitor the verran. When there was no forage, he had it shipped to Sylvawyld. When the nut harvest was meager, he had more shipped there. They lived wild, but were protected and defended. And always there was an inventory before the hunt, and much consultation as to what the kill could be." She smiled. "There were no accidents on my father's hunts."

It was exactly the way his dad had managed the boar population, and Troy felt an unexpected sense of understanding with her. "My dad let the sounder roam over a larger area than the farm, but they were fenced. Sometimes someone let a male loose or hunted without permission." He frowned. "When I came back after my dad's death, I didn't see any boar. I assumed my dad had sold or killed the sounder, but maybe they were in the forest the whole time." It was an intriguing thought, but he couldn't hunt them. There wasn't time.

Drakina shook her head and climbed the steps to the porch behind him. "They are wily, if they are like verran, and they are obstinate. Worthy adversaries for they are not readily killed."

"No, they aren't."

"I would not be surprised if they survived wild." She surveyed the house. "You grew up here?"

"I did." The key was in the mailbox, just as it

always had been. Troy had it in his hand before he realized that the boar offered the perfect opportunity to fulfill both their dreams. He turned to face Drakina. "Do you want to hunt?"

Her eyes lit with pleasure. "The verran?"

"Sure." Troy couldn't see why not and the prospect gave her obvious pleasure.

She exhaled, her eyes glittering. "I should love to hunt verran again!" Her eyes narrowed and she winced. "But other Terrans will see me. It would not be right to reveal myself in dragon form and disrupt the assumptions of your kind."

"Princess! Remember who you're talking to!"

Her lips parted and she breathed the word. "MindBender. Can you shield me from view?"

"I can convince them that they aren't seeing what they think they are."

"But how? I will fly too fast for you to follow, even on your Harley, and it might not be able to make a path through the forest." She wrinkled her nose. "The sound will frighten them, as well, and reveal your presence."

Troy's heart was leaping at the obvious solution. "No, no Harley. Take me with you."

She eyed him. "I must have my claws free to hunt. I cannot carry you."

"But I can ride on your back." Troy couldn't believe he was being given this opportunity. "Come on, princess. Take me for a dragon ride."

"And we shall hunt verran together!" she declared and flung herself into his arms. She flattened him against the wall and kissed him with such enthusiasm that Troy was torn between a hunt and a seduction.

Then Drakina leapt off the porch in her exuberance and shifted shape in a blinding halo of light. "Fetch a rope, Carrier! We ride to hunt!"

The Carrier brought her a gift beyond expectation.

Other cultures might dance when they courted a mate. Some shared meals with a prospective partner. But the dragons of Incendium had always weighed the valor of a mate and the suitability of a companion in his or her lust for the hunt.

Drakina was not going to be shown lacking.

She instructed Troy as to how to best fasten the rope about her dragon form, so that it would offer a secure grip for him but not restrain her. He still had to hang on and to hook his legs through the rope, but she liked the feel of him upon her shoulders. She felt that she carried a precious burden and knew she had to remember to safeguard him.

She was well aware of his awe and his pleasure.

When she took flight, she felt his quick intake of breath. Because it was new for him, the flight was new for her. She savored it as she seldom did, noting how wondrous it felt when often she took her powers for granted.

"First, an inventory," she said, then followed the scent of a solitary male. It didn't take long to find him, for he was close, and she flew low so that Troy could see him closely.

"He's an old boy, maybe nine or ten years," he said. "Look at those tusks."

The verran cast a baleful eye at Drakina, but she

ascended, seeking the others before the choice was made. She found five more solitary male boars, spread over a large range. Troy told her that his family's lands were adjacent to a park, and two of the boar had escaped into that area. They all appeared to be eating well.

She then sought the sounder of females. There were six of them, with a cluster of young being protected by the mothers. There seemed to be two groups of young ones, one group much bigger than the others. The small ones were striped and not very big at all.

They were adorable.

"A late litter," Troy said. "Still nursing."

"Oh! They are so small!" Drakina turned a circuit high in the air, yearning. "Are they soft?" she asked quietly.

"Do you want to find out?"

Drakina felt her pulse quicken. "Can you MindBend such creatures?" Truly her mate offered bountiful gifts!

"Sure. It's how we used to corral them, although no one knew how it worked but me. My dad just thought I had a gift."

Drakina supposed that MindBending might be a gift, not a liability. The Carrier certainly had explored its advantages.

"I would like that very much," she confessed.

"Then let's do it. Leave me in a tree, just in case the MindBend slips." Drakina heard him chuckle. "I know I can't outrun an angry boar."

He might be trying to charm her. Drakina didn't care. She chose a tall and strong tree and left him high in its boughs. Then she shifted shape, clinging to the branches at his side. She listened as he explained their annual cycle. By this point in the Terran year, the young should all have been weaned.

The sows were aware of them, for more than one glanced upward, but they were remarkably untroubled. Drakina guessed that each of them weighed twice or even three times as much as she, and they would be formidable opponents. They would be at their most powerful if they believed their young to be threatened.

She waited until Troy cast her a smile. "We're good," he murmured. "Go."

Drakina descended the tree slowly and steadily, ensuring that she made as little noise as possible. The sounder did not move away, but continued to forage nearby. She smiled when she heard the little ones squeak when they believed they were too far from their mothers. She watched as two latched on to nurse and her heart swelled.

What fine small creatures they were.

What fierce adults they would be.

Her feet were on the ground before she doubted the Carrier's words in the least. The largest sow lifted her head and surveyed Drakina, her dark eyes small and her gaze intent. She would be the matriarch of the sounder. Drakina's heart stopped and she hoped the Carrier was right about his skills. Then the sow returned to her foraging. She dug in the ground with her snout and loosed a root, chewing on it noisily as she moved slowly onward. Three squeakers followed her, one latched on to a nipple even as she strolled and two hovering in her considerable shadow.

They were the smaller ones. Drakina counted the squeakers and wished to ask Troy whether they were usually more fertile than this. They might not be faring as well in the wild as could be hoped.

She could have turned back, but Drakina wanted to touch one. It might be the only chance she ever had to touch a young boar, the closest creature to a verran. She flicked a glance at Troy, still perched in the tree. He gave her a hand signal, his thumb pointed upward, which she didn't understand, but his confident smile told her all she needed to know.

She moved forward stealthily, her heart in her throat.

It would be so easy.

Even as he exuded calm thoughts toward the boars, Troy knew he could stop his MindBend. He could let the sows realize the danger posed by a woman approaching them and let them complete his assignment for him. Even if Drakina could shift shape fast enough to defend herself, he didn't imagine she could fend off six furious boars at once.

They were fierce and fast. They could do his dirty work. He certainly wouldn't have been able to stop them once they attacked.

But there was no question of him betraying his dragon princess. Drakina was so enchanted with the young boar, and he liked the way that delight lit her expression. Plus she had given him a dragon ride, making one of his oldest dreams come true. It would just be wrong to put her in danger.

It was right to give her something in return.

She reached the sounder and the largest of the

sows grunted as it glared at her. He couldn't MindBend them into complete oblivion but they were calm. Drakina moved slowly and carefully, which helped a lot. Troy saw that she had gathered some berries while she moved closer and she let them fall on the ground ahead of her.

One of the smaller squeakers peeked out from beneath its mother with curiosity. It was striped and furry, about the size of a basketball and nearly as round. It peered at Drakina, then at the berries, and sniffed, cautious but interested.

She waited, more still than he could have believed possible.

He kept his MindBend locked on the sows, particularly the biggest one. She was not only matriarch but the mother of the curious squeaker.

The mother took another step away from Drakina, ambling toward the denser scrub around the perimeter of the clearing. The little one looked between its mother and Drakina, then made a dash for the berries. It devoured one, hesitated, then sought the others. Troy guessed that they were gone when the squeaker considered Drakina.

She slowly stretched out her hand. Even at this height, he could see that there were more berries in it.

The squeaker's nose twitched.

Troy waited, rather than giving it a nudge.

He smiled when it surrendered to temptation and went to Drakina. As it ate, she cautiously stretched out her other hand and stroked its back. The mother made a grunt that was a summons, the little one finished the berries, then bolted after the big sow.

The sounder moved into the denser undergrowth, unhurried but charting a course away from Drakina.

She stood and pivoted, her triumphant smile almost blinding Troy in it brightness. He found himself grinning in return, then she leapt into the air and shifted shape. She snatched him from the tree and soared high in the sky. Her excitement was contagious and he found himself laughing as she raced through the air, turned a somersault, soared toward the sun, then dove to fly low over the forest again. She spiraled down to a rocky outcropping, shifted shape just before her feet touched the ground and backed him against a tree. Her eyes were sparkling.

"Troy!" she exclaimed. "Thank you!" And she kissed him with such enthusiasm that he had no chance to say anything for a long time.

Drakina might have celebrated on that rock, in the open air, but Troy caught her shoulders in his hands and broke their kiss. He wasn't unaffected, but perhaps he was shy. "I thought you wanted to hunt," he said, with a gleam in his eye. "First things, first, princess."

"I will say that your slow and thorough scheme has its advantages," she said, unable to be vexed with him at all.

"The longer the burn, the hotter the flames," he said.

She arched a brow. "We shall see."

"We will." He was cocky again and she couldn't help smiling at his attitude. "So, what about those boar?"

"They are wonderful. Healthy animals and much like verran. I think they may not have sufficient feed on their own, though."

"The litters are small," he agreed. "I remember them having eight or even ten squeakers in a litter."

"Did you smell it?" she asked, guessing the answer as soon as she uttered the words. "The litters were all sired by the oldest boar. His scent is strong in their blood."

"You can smell that?"

"My kind have a refined sense of smell, Carrier." Drakina considered the forest spread before them and couldn't help being reminded of Sylvawyld and its joys. "This is a fine place. You are fortunate to have had such a home."

He nodded, following her gaze. "I couldn't wait to get away, but it's good to come back."

She smiled, glad he had shared his homecoming with her. "What is your thinking about this population?"

"I have ideas. Let's see if we think the same way. Tell me what your father would do," he invited.

Drakina didn't hesitate. "My father would hunt the oldest male on this day, to encourage diversity in the lineage of the sounder."

"That would be my choice, too."

"Beyond that, the sows and young must be protected so that the herd can grow. And the other males must be encouraged to return to your family's fenced lands, for their protection and that of other Terrans." She pursed her lips. "There may be a late litter for the same reason that the litters are small, because the sounder has nutritional needs that are unsatisfied. Once they are back on your family lands, I would supplement their diet." She looked at Troy. "And you?"

He smiled. "I would do exactly the same thing, princess. Are you up for hunting that old boar?"

Drakina smiled. "His pelt is as good as mine."

Although he had always wanted to ride a dragon, and although he had often imagined what it would be like, the reality was far beyond his dreams. The second time that Drakina carried him aloft, Troy was less overwhelmed and could compare dream and reality better.

A dragon ride was simply magical.

Drakina was all muscle. She made flying look effortless but Troy could feel the power of her body beneath him. Her dragon scales seemed to be black, but when touched by sun, he could see that they glimmered in a hundred shades of metallic green. Her wings were like black leather, and they stretched wide, sending a current of wind at him when she flapped them hard. Her eyes were a glittering jade. Her talons were gold, as well as long and sharp. With the wind in his hair and Drakina warm beneath him, Troy felt like the king of the world.

And that had been his impression before she touched the squeaker.

Before he'd seen the compassion that mingled with her ferocity.

Before he saw the woman in the dragon.

When she snatched him up and soared through the sky, triumphant, Troy felt alive as he never had before. It had taken everything in him to break their kiss, then the hunt had been a challenge and a thrill. The old boar had been as cunning and fierce as Drakina had predicted.

But she had won.

And Troy had had a front row seat.

It was dusk when they returned to the house. Troy led Drakina to the bunker where his father had always cleaned his kill. It was a lot easier to deal with the boar's weight with Drakina helping in her dragon form. He cleaned the carcass as she watched and hung it to cure in the cool dark space, only realizing once he was done that there might not ever be anyone to eat it.

The wager demanded that he kill Drakina to survive. If Troy succeeded in that, he'd have no taste for the boar, much less the memories it would conjure of this hunt.

If he didn't kill Drakina, he would be executed himself.

Troy felt trapped. Were they only destined to have this short time together? What about her astrologer's prediction of their shared destiny? What about the son who was supposed to be conceived?

Maybe the astrologers had seen that Troy might let Drakina survive, regardless of the price to himself. It was the noble thing to do, but he wanted more.

He wanted more time with his dragon princess.

A bleak sense of despair filled his heart, but Drakina's hand landed on his shoulder. He turned to find her smiling at him. "It is the way of life," she said gently, and he realized she'd mistaken the reason for his reaction. "We all must die in our time, and it is the responsibility of the gamekeeper to manage the herd for their own health and welfare." She surveyed the boar. "He was majestic. He was robust and virile. He sired many, and his days of life were both numerous and good. He was a champion to the end. We must celebrate him and his life."

"Don't you mourn what is lost?"

Drakina considered his question for a moment before she replied. "It is right to feel sadness when confronted with change, but there is only cause to mourn when the loss is untimely." She took his hand. "Or when matters have been left incomplete. Come, Troy, celebrate with me and finish what we have begun." She leaned close and swept her lips over his, giving him an enticing taste of her kiss.

That was when he knew. Given the choices, there was only one he could make.

He could give her the son she wanted, the crown prince who was foretold to save her world, and accept the consequences to himself for not winning the wager.

And Drakina would never know the truth.

Fulfilling her desire and protecting her from the truth would be the choice of a champion.

His choice.

Troy locked his arms around Drakina and swept her into his arms, slanting his mouth over hers and kissing her deeply. She made a little purr of pleasure and twined her arms around his neck, her passion igniting his desire all over again. If making love with Drakina was to be the last deed Troy did, he would make it a celebration to remember.

Chapter Four

The Carrier appeared to have abandoned the notion of 'slowly and thoroughly'.

He carried Drakina to the house, kicking the door closed behind them and continued to a chamber with large windows overlooking the forest. There was a large hearth on one wall, made of rounded river stones, though there was no need for a fire in this season. The rug was thick and the cushions were plentiful. He bore her down to the floor in the middle of the room, crushing her a little beneath his weight as he kissed her with uncharacteristic haste.

His passion fed her own and made Drakina impatient to feel his strength inside her. She ran her hands over his shoulders and down his back, then rolled him over so that she was astride him.

"Why do I get the feeling that you like to be in charge?" he teased, before she made sure he couldn't ask any more questions. Her mouth was locked upon his, her tongue dancing with his, her hands busy with that cursed fastening on his jeans. She finally stripped them off and cast them aside, then tugged open his shirt.

Troy rolled her to her back and straddled her as he removed the shirt. Drakina surveyed him with great satisfaction. She liked this frenzy in him, this need to claim her for his own. She reached for his erection, but he evaded her fingers, sliding down to unfasten her jeans. His eyes shone as he relieved her of them, flinging them aside with similar abandon.

Drakina tore open the front of her shirt and wriggled out of it. She preened at the admiration in his gaze. In a moment more, they were both completely nude.

"Your way this time, princess," he said, his words thrumming with intent. "Next time, mine."

"And the time after that?" she teased

His eyes lit with an appealing humor. "We'll have to negotiate."

Drakina laughed that he shared her assumption that there would be at least three couplings. Then he bent over her and kissed her nipple with exquisite deliberation. He caught the tight peak between his lips and teased it to an impossibly tight point, then flicking his tongue across it so that Drakina cried out with pleasure. Again, he caught her hands in his and held her wrists together as he tormented her with pleasure. She liked being held captive by this warrior; she liked better that she was compelled to accept every sensation he chose to grant.

She was writhing on the rug by the time he lowered himself over her. She arched her back and parted her lips when she felt him against her.

"You're so wet," he whispered against her throat.

"I have been awaiting you," she replied and saw

the flash of his smile before he eased into her. They both froze when he was completely sheathed and their gazes locked in keen awareness of each other.

Drakina licked her lips. "Perfect fit," she whispered.

"Kismet?" he asked, lifting a brow as if he didn't believe it.

Drakina laughed and tore her hands free of his grasp. She seized his buttocks and parted her legs, drawing him deeper inside, wanting all he had to give. Troy shook a little in his surprise, then he braced himself above her and began to move. His erection dragged against her clitoris and Drakina wanted to roar with pleasure—when she saw the twinkle in his eyes, she knew he moved this way deliberately. She smiled up at him. "It seems you cannot abandon the notion of slow and thorough," she teased.

He buried himself within her and rolled his hips. "I want to watch you come," he said. "I felt it last time, but this time, I want to watch."

"What happened to fast and furious?"

"After you come," he vowed. "Then I won't be able to hold back."

"Promises, promises," Drakina complained but she was only teasing him. She'd never experienced such a splendid mating before.

It was due to her partner. Troy's confidence, his skill, his size, all combined to make her see the merit of slow and thorough. She rolled her hips, trying to draw him even deeper inside, and felt him get harder. She massaged her own nipples, seeing how his eyes glittered, and writhed beneath him. Troy rolled them over so that she was above him and she shook out her hair. She kept pinching her own nipples, ensuring that he had a fine view, and rolled her hips so that she rubbed against him.

When she moaned at the size and strength of him, Troy eased his finger and thumb between them, then teased her clitoris. He rolled it, then pinched it hard, so hard that she came in a sudden rush. Drakina gasped, she shook, and then she roared with the vigor of her release.

For the first time, she wished it had taken a little longer.

"You make me yearn for slow and thorough," she complained.

Troy chuckled with satisfaction. He rolled her beneath him and drove deep inside her. He bent to capture her lips and plundered her mouth, even as he claimed her with sufficient speed and passion to satisfy her impatience. Drakina felt the thunder of his heart, the haste of his breathing, the quickening of everything within him. Her own body responded and she felt the tide rise anew within her, redoubling its power, filling her with heat and promise.

Until he drove deeper than ever and roared with his release. Drakina came again and clutched at him, holding him fast against her as their combined shouts made the floor shake beneath them.

She tasted salt on his temple and felt the Seed run hot inside her.

It was done.

When Troy lifted his head, she smiled up at him and ran a hand through his hair with pride. The Seed was within her. The Crown Prince would be conceived within hours. Incendium would be saved, by some means she could not name, and she would be free of her father's command. Drakina had a strange sensation of her heart feeling full enough to burst, and yet it was none of those things that gave her such pleasure.

It was Troy, looking at her with admiration and more than a little desire. Troy, who had been driven by seeing her passion to make his amorous claim with haste and power. Troy, the warrior who would be the father of her son.

Drakina's throat was tight, but it wasn't because of the son he had given her.

Kismet. She thought of the word that had been repeated between them, and her gaze fell to the tattoo on his arm. Had she found her HeartKeeper?

The fact was that her quest was accomplished. She could leave immediately. She had achieved all that was necessary. Yet, she wanted to linger.

She wanted to stay with Troy.

Was there a greater destiny between them? It was one thing to be the Carrier of the Seed. It was another to be her destined mate. But her HeartKeeper? Drakina had never imagined she would be so fortunate as to have such a partner in her life.

But in this moment, she suspected that he lay atop her, disheveled and most satisfied. She reached up and framed his face in her hands, then drew him down for a leisurely kiss. Her heart was full. There were no words. There was only flesh against flesh, pleasure, exquisite torment, and thundering release.

All because of the marvel that was Troy.

Her HeartKeeper.

Troy knew he shouldn't have been surprised that Drakina had sexual stamina to match his own.

She was a dragon shifter, after all.

After she had blown his mind, he tugged on his jeans and went down to the basement and turn on the water again. He got the old water tank going, then primed the pump for the well. He flushed the pipes, impressed that the plumbing was still in pretty good shape.

He went back to the living room to find that Drakina had lit a fire on the hearth. She was naked, and evidently at ease to be so. She was standing at the window looking over the forest behind the farm. Dusk was falling, and the light outside was beautiful. "Always my favorite time of day," he said without meaning to do so.

"Why?"

"Because the sky is still colored from the sunset, but you can see the stars high overhead. In the east, it looks like night already. And I like that light blue, the last greenish bit before the sky gets dark. It seems magical." He frowned, uncertain he could explain it properly. "Like we're on the threshold of something."

"Neither day nor night," Drakina agreed. She reached for him and he went to her side, drawing him into her arms as they looked together at the forest. "Does this time have a name?"

"Twilight."

She said the word, then nodded approval. "It is a threshold, except that you have no choice but to go forward into night. You cannot go back to the day."

Her words seemed portentous and she was more serious than he'd seen her before. "Sometimes you just have to walk through the shadow to the light."

She turned a little in his embrace so she could meet his gaze. "I believe that is almost always true." Her gaze searched his. "Have you secrets, Troy?"

"Everyone has secrets, princess." He averted his gaze. "Shower?"

"Is that a manner of bathing?"

"And one that lends itself well to what I have in mind," he promised, then led her to the large bathroom on the second floor. The shower was roomy enough for two, and the hot water tank seemed to want to make up for its long rest.

It turned out that Drakina was more than amenable to learning more about leisurely lovemaking.

How could Drakina have ever imagined that her mate was unattractive? Troy was perfect, just the way he was. A valiant warrior, built strong and true. A man sufficiently confident to challenge her, a dragon shifter.

And that smile could have been designed to drive Drakina wild.

His nature was good and kind, noble even, as was fitting for the Carrier of the Seed. His sexual endurance was phenomenal. His son would be strong and potent, a majestic crown prince. The combination of gifts from both parents would make him formidable.

Maybe he could save Incendium. Drakina was

surprised to realize that she cared less about that than she had.

Was Troy her HeartKeeper?

In addition to his other gifts, he made love like a champion. His touch curled her toes and exhausted her, yet left her hungry for more. She could become used to him by her side.

She touched her lips to Troy's shoulder, thinking of defying her father about the Carrier becoming the Consort, and Troy stirred in his sleep.

He smiled and opened his eyes, looking rumpled, satisfied and adorable. Drakina's heart squeezed. "Sleep well?" he murmured.

"Long enough," she replied, moving into his embrace. He tangled his fingers in her hair, surveying her with admiration. "Perhaps we should ensure the Seed is planted."

"Don't you know?"

She smiled that he understood her so well. "It is," she admitted. "The Crown Prince is conceived." She ran her hands over his skin lightly. "But it would not hurt to be absolutely sure."

He laughed. "You're a fantasy come true."

"How so?"

"I think every man dreams of having a beautiful partner who is insatiable, too."

"But probably not a dragon shifter."

"You might be surprised, princess." He pulled her head down and kissed her slowly, easily summoning her passion again.

"Did you fantasize about such a partner?" she asked when Troy finally let her speak.

That smile turned mischievous. "Come on. I'll

show you something." He seized a towel and knotted it around his waist, then rolled out of bed, grabbing her hand. He led her upstairs, to the part of the house she hadn't yet seen, and into a small chamber toward the back. There were stars on the ceiling and maps pinned to the walls, a model space ship hanging from a string, and a shelf filled with books. A small bed was in the corner, a desk in the other, and she realized this was a child's room.

"Mine," he said, anticipating her question.

His. Troy had lived in this room as a boy. Drakina studied it, wanting to memorize every detail and know all about his childhood. He seemed disinclined to talk, though. He was kneeling in the far corner, by the window, and had pulled back the rug. One of the floorboards had been cut and he lifted it up, revealing a hiding place nestled beneath the floor.

His face lit when he reached in and withdrew a square tin box with a lid. It was covered with a plaid design and marked with the logo of a shortbread company. Shortbread. Drakina wondered what that was. This seemed a most strange place to keep any kind of food.

Troy set the tin on the carpet with obvious pleasure. "My treasury," he confessed, a twinkle in his eye. "Or my hoard."

Drakina smiled and sat opposite him, wrapped in her own towel. "The secrets of the heart are in the hoard," she said, her tone teasing. "Are you sure you want to show me?"

He nodded once, pried the lid off the tin and handed it to her.

Inside were three small model cars. There was a

ball made of pieces of string tied together and wound into a ball. She lifted it and turned it in her hand, mystified, then met his gaze.

"I needed a rope if I was ever going to ride a dragon," he admitted.

Drakina lifted the chunk of rock with amethyst crystals on one side and gave him another look.

"And I needed a gift for her. Something shiny." He smiled. "Gems seemed a good choice."

Drakina smiled. There was another rock, one that was dull and grey, shaped like a cone.

"A genuine dragon tooth," Troy confided.

"It is not." She turned it, seeing that it was also the shape of a fang.

"I was sure it was. It was proof that there were dragons out there in the hills."

"Maybe there are."

"There was one, and that's good enough for me." They shared another of those sizzling smiles and Drakina's heart skipped a beat.

HeartKeeper.

There was another piece of rock, a sliver of obsidian, that caught the light and was filled with reflections. It was almost round, about the size of her palm.

"My father brought me that. He said it was a dragon scale and I treasured it."

Drakina smiled, both at the whimsy of a man who would tell a child a tale he did not believe, and the fact that the rock was almost the same color as her own dragon scales. Could her father and his astrologers be right about destiny? "Where did he find it?"

"He said it was on the path to the barn, which I found very exciting."

"The dragon had been in your yard!"

"Exactly." Troy lifted it from her hand and turned it in the light. "I suspect, though, that he bought it or maybe even had it shaped, just to thrill me."

They shared a smile at that. "Peri, my youngest sister, found a story in my father's archives about mice that fulfilled wishes," she said. "We have no mice on Incendium, and those on Regalia do not fulfill wishes. They are considered a pest there."

"A lot of people feel that way about them here, too."

"But my father indulged Peri and shared her wonder over the story. Together, they conspired to steal small pieces of cheese from the kitchen—because the castellan does not tolerate food being eaten in our chambers—and set them out each night in her chamber to lure the wish-granting mice."

"Did they ever see any?"

"Never, for there are none. But the cheese disappeared each night, which thrilled Peri."

Troy grinned. "Your father ate it?"

"He would never admit it, but I saw him once, leaving her chamber with a plate of small pieces of cheese."

"You don't think it's bad to encourage kids' fantasies then?"

"Who is to say what is fantasy and what is truth?" Drakina leaned closer and brushed her lips across Troy's. "Your father probably thought there were no dragons, but he was wrong." She touched her lips to his once more, and whispered. "I like that you dreamed of dragons. It makes me think that the astrologers were right, and that there is something to be said in favor of destiny."

"I wanted to be a dragon more than anything else in the world," he admitted, putting away his box of treasures.

"Maybe being the father of one is almost as good," she murmured, and then there was little more to be said for quite a while.

Troy awakened in the guest bedroom with Drakina sleeping beside him. He'd forgotten how quiet it was at the farm, and how tranquil. He laid in the darkness for a long time, listening to the wind and feeling Drakina's breath against his shoulder. He was tired, but in a good way. He'd never made love to a woman so many times in a row, or in such rapid succession. They'd done it in the living room, as fast and hard as she wanted, then slower the next time. He'd had her against the wall of the shower and again on the bathroom floor, and once more in the bed. He'd never imagined he could do that and still want more.

His dragon princess had a gift for challenging his assumptions.

Her hair was cast over them, glinting with inner light even in the shadows. It might have been made of flame, or a conduit for it. Troy smoothed it back from her forehead, wishing he had time to learn all about her.

But his two days were over. They'd be coming for him by midday.

Drakina would need something to eat.

The house had been empty for years, but his mother had canned and stockpiled in preparation for the Apocalypse. And his father had stored wine. Troy was sure there was more that was still good to eat. It might be a strange meal, but it would be a generous one.

His last meal, or at least the last one that counted.

It was not the nature of Drakina's kind to sleep deeply. The dragons of Incendium dozed by habit, particularly when they were not surrounded by their own household and bodyguards. Drakina smiled to herself as Troy's fingertips danced over her flesh, and she welcomed his ongoing exploration. She feigned sleep while he toyed with her hair and considered how best to pleasure him before he left the bed.

But he rose abruptly and strode toward the chamber for washing.

Drakina opened one eye, just a slit, to savor the view of him walking away. She had yet to see her mate fully naked, for Troy seemed inclined to wrap fabric around his hips or don his jeans or seduce her in darkness. She deserved one good look.

Perhaps more.

Could she change her father's thinking about her having a Terran Consort? It would not be easy to leave Troy and return home.

The view was every bit as fine as Drakina anticipated, Troy's lean muscled strength kindling her passion anew. His skin was pale gold, tanned slightly and all over, so he couldn't be that shy. There was a

mark at the base of his spine, too elaborate to be a
birthmark, to dark to be naturally wrought. She
peered at it and her heart stopped in dismay.

A tattoo.

Not just any tattoo. A distinctive blue whorl of
triangles.

She recognized the symbol well. It was the mark
of a condemned man in the penal colony of Xanto.

No one escaped that place alive.

Unless they were released on a bet, as sport for
the rich of the galaxy.

Drakina barely managed to keep from gasping
aloud. Troy closed the bathroom door and Drakina
heard the water running. She rolled to her back and
stared at the ceiling, her heart racing.

Could she love a condemned man?

Could she love a condemned man who had
deceived her? Because if Troy had been incarcerated
on Xanto, then he had left Terra and returned. He
was not just a Terran and not just a MindBender.
Could he have tricked her?

Drakina recalled how Troy had been unsurprised
by her nature and her abilities. She recalled her sense
that he recognized her when she walked into the bar,
as if he had been waiting for her. She recalled his
reluctant confession that he was a MindBender and
that he had been in her mind twice. Twice? Or just
the once when she caught him—and he'd known the
rest about her because he wasn't the Terran she'd
thought he was.

She bit her lip and considered the power of his
gift. A mother boar could not be easy to beguile.

Troy was not just any MindBender.

Drakina was afraid she knew which one he was.

Had the notion that he might be her HeartKeeper been her own thought? Or one provided for her? Why?

She rolled over to her belly and seized her computer. She tapped as long as the water ran, seeking the answers to her questions and giving fuel to her suspicions. By the time Troy opened the door again, she was sitting on the bed, her hair braided, waiting for him.

He was wearing his jeans and had a towel looped over his shoulders. He was surprised to see her awake, but his smile revealed that he was pleased. He took a step toward her as if to resume their lovemaking but she halted him with her words.

"You have not told me your great secret, Carrier," she said with quiet heat.

"Carrier again?" he mused. He folded his arms across his chest. "I'm guessing that's not a good sign."

Drakina put the computer down. "I do not like to be deceived."

He paled then and shoved a hand through his hair. His expression turned grim and she was relieved that he didn't tell her a lie.

"What have you done?" she demanded. "Why were you sentenced to the penal colony of Xanto?"

His lips set mutinously. He was not surprised, though. "I was caught."

"Caught doing what?"

"Caught doing what my owner commanded me to do. A slave doesn't have any choice, Drakina. And a slave sold to a gang of thieves has even less of one.

I had to do what I did to survive."

A gang of thieves?

"Were you sold to the Gloria Furora?" she asked in awe.

The simmering anger in his eyes was all the answer she needed, and Drakina felt a wave of sympathy for him.

"I'm amazed that you *did* survive that pack of thieves and counterfeiters. They are not known for being tolerant of any strangers or slaves."

He scooped up a shirt and tugged it over his shoulders while she considered him.

"You lied to me about being Terran."

He shook his head. "No. I am Terran. You assumed I had never left Terra, which is a different thing."

"Did you MindBend me twice?"

He winced. "*That* was a lie. Only the once and you caught me."

"So you did know about me before we met."

"Of course. It was part of the deal, princess."

Drakina wasn't sure she was ready to know about the deal. "Did you lie about your name?" She had to ask.

"No. It's always been Troy. I didn't lie about my family or my history, princess. It was all real, all except the deal I had to make to survive." He gave her an intent look. "I was forbidden to mention it to you, for obvious reasons."

So, he had made a bet to save his own life. "The gamblers on Xanto."

Troy nodded. "They offered a wager. If I could win, I could live."

"And if not, you would die." Drakina took a deep breath, because she'd found more. "The most expensive commodities traded in the sentient slave markets of Naruhm are MindBenders."

Troy held her gaze as if daring her to say it out loud.

Drakina dared. "The equivalent of twenty solar years ago in Terran time, the confederation initiated a search for MindBenders throughout the galaxy, declaring all planets to be eligible hunting grounds." She swallowed. "They launched a thousand ships."

His brows rose. "I didn't think you'd know that story."

"My father collects stories. It is his contention that the same tales or elements circulate through all cultures in the universe, manifesting in a multitude of ways, yet remaining true to their essence." She pursed her lips. "He would say that your destiny was defined when you were born, and that your name was chosen to mirror that fate."

"But my mother didn't read classical history. I don't think she knew that story."

"It does not have to be a conscious choice. The name could have come to her in a dream, or she might have been alerted to it in another way." Drakina was dismissive of the notion. "One of my father's astrologers or scholars could explain it better than me." She fixed him with a look. "Of greater import is your story. The equivalent of ten solar years ago in Terran time, there were rumors that the pirates of Manganus Five offered a MindBender for sale on the shadow market. They refused to reveal where they had found the MindBender in question so he or she could not be trade freely. If that MindBender existed, he was never heard from again."

Troy smiled his crooked smile. "Who says no one really disappears in the galaxy." His tone was wry and Drakina knew he didn't expect an answer.

"Who offered you the chance to escape the prison colony of Xanto?" she asked. "And what do you have to do to win your freedom?"

Troy sighed. He shoved a hand through his hair, but she sensed the defeat within him. "All you really need to know is that I won't be doing it, princess," he said, his voice rough. His gaze was bright and bored into hers. "I've decided to lose."

"I still want to know."

"And I want breakfast. Come on. Food first."

It was a suggestion that Drakina found difficult to dispute. Troy had kept every promise he had made thus far.

She chose to believe he would do as much again.

But she dressed before she followed him, to show him that their intimacy was at an end. Even if he was her HeartKeeper, his truth made a future between them impossible.

Going down into the cellar was like being punched in the gut. The small cold room was filled with memories of Troy's mother, and just as crowded with her preserves. He found pickles and jam, wine, and sealed tins of crispbread. The locked and even colder room beyond still had the scent of smoked ham.

He found a last one, hanging from the ceiling, as

well as a wheel of cheese, sealed in wax and locked in a tin. He brought it all into the kitchen and began to assemble a meal.

He opened the wine, knowing he wouldn't have to wait long for Drakina.

He was right.

He was carving the ham, which was still perfect, when he heard the tread of her footfall. "They found me here," he said, seeing no reason to beat around the bush. "Alone on the farm. My mom had died and then my dad. I'd lived in town for a while after my mom passed. I had a job at old man Wilcox's garage and I liked it. I worked a lot, because it was better than thinking. I only came back here once in a blue moon."

Of course, Drakina frowned. "Terra's moon is not blue."

"It's an expression. It means not very often, because every once in a while, our moon looks blue from here."

She spared a glance at the sky, but the moon had set hours before. The sun was rising.

"When my dad was gone, the farm wasn't the same. It had always been quiet, but it was lonely. He'd sold the last of the pigs, and like I said, I thought he'd sold the boar, too. I closed it all up and went back to town to work. I came back at intervals to check on the place, and I was here when they came."

She sat on a stool and watched him as she listened.

"I'd never seen anything like that tracking beam." He shook his head. "It was like a ray of starlight."

"You should not have seen it. Terra is among those colonies lacking sufficient sophistication for interference."

"I couldn't stay away from it either."

"They laced it to lure you, then. A trap." Drakina tapped her fingertips. "That's why you were sold on the shadow market. It was illegal for them to harvest you here. Without provenance, they couldn't sell you in the legitimate slave markets."

"I hope they got less than I was worth," he said and heard his bitterness.

Drakina's smile was sad. "It was probably still worth their trouble. You were said to be the greatest MindBender in the galaxy."

Troy shrugged, uncertain how to respond to her admiration. "I didn't know what the beam was. I saw it. I was drawn to it. I stepped into its light, and that was it. Next I knew, I was on a ship, in what I realized was a prison cell."

"Then sold at auction," she guessed, sympathy in her eyes. "To the Gloria Furora. Truly, Troy, you could not have had worse luck. What did they do with you?"

"Hired me out as an assassin. I was either locked up, hunting someone or making a kill."

"Also against galactic law," Drakina murmured softly. He didn't know whether she was disappointed in him or displeased by his treatment.

He nodded, not proud of what he had done. "I defied them a couple of times, but they're inventive bastards."

"No one survives the torture of the Gloria Furora. They have a consuming hatred of all others."

"Thanks. I feel like less of a loser knowing that."

"And so you were caught, doing what?"

Troy winced. "Assassinating one of the warrior maidens of Cumae."

Her eyes widened and he knew he'd lost her support. "No! The culprit was never found!"

"Oh yes, he was."

"But the trial would be in the record..."

"Not the way the Gloria Furora play the game. They delivered me, paid for a conviction and I went mining. The person who caught me disappeared without a trade."

Her eyes were wide.

"They have a reputation to protect, apparently."

"Not that," she whispered.

Troy frowned. She looked truly shaken.

"Who was your target?"

"Her name was Arista..." At Drakina's gasp of horror, Troy stopped. Her expression made him fear the worst. "Friend of yours?"

Drakina turned away, but not so quickly that he didn't see her tears. "Arista was the best friend of my sister Gemma. She was well loved in our home and still deeply mourned."

And Troy had been the one to kill her.

He was pretty sure Drakina wasn't going to be having their son any more, not if she had anything to say about it.

He might as well nail his own coffin shut. "Like I said, I was snared and delivered to the court, then condemned and sent to the penal colonies of Xanto. The sentence was for me to mine for sixteen quartos, then be executed." Troy grimaced. "They like to give prisoners time to realize just how screwed they are."

"And so it was until the gamblers came." Drakina's voice was hard and he looked up to see that her eyes were cold. Her arms were folded across her chest, as if she needed one more barrier against him. "What was the wager?" she asked, though he was sure she'd already guessed.

"My life for yours." He put the platter of ham on the counter between them and watched her nostrils flare. "Pretty simple really, or it should have been."

"What is that to mean?"

"That I'm not going to do it. I'm giving you my promise, and you know I'll keep it."

She frowned. "Then you'll die."

"I have it on good authority that we all do, and the only deaths worth mourning are the untimely ones." He couldn't look at her as he continued. "I'd rather try to be a champion, princess, although I might not have much chance to succeed." He dared to flick a glance her way. The hair was standing up on the back of his neck and he knew in his heart that they'd returned for him. "I'm going to lose the wager, but you have the Seed, and if the prophecy is right, the crown prince will save Incendium. Winner take all." He saluted her and moved toward the door. The tracking beam was illuminating the same spot in the yard as it had all those years before. "You might want to find out who wants you dead, princess. It might be Prince Urbanus, or he might be acting for someone else."

"You can't go!"

"I have to go. We both know it." Troy paused in the doorway, looking back one last time, knowing the sight of her would be with him to the very end. "I love you, Drakina," he admitted, his voice husky. "Maybe, just maybe, you'll tell the kid something good about me."

Then he turned and strode to the beam. The light washed over him, making him tingle to his very marrow. Troy could almost feel his electrons being shaken apart and cast into the sky. He closed his eyes, knowing it would be over all too soon.

The last thing he thought he heard was Drakina calling his name, but Troy knew that had to be wishful thinking.

He was just yearning for what could never be.

What manner of judge condemned a slave for fulfilling a command?

Drakina had her suspicions, but she would unravel the truth. She knew she could not defeat any party sent to retrieve Troy, not alone. She took the meat that so resembled verran and packed the feast her mate had prepared for her. Then she transported herself home to Incendium with haste. Once in the royal palace, she strode down the corridors to the library and demanded that the portals be secured.

She had no time to speak with her family.

She had no time to reassure her father, or whisper with her sisters.

The crown prince was conceived. Her duty to her father was done. Her independence was won.

And if Troy's life was to be saved, Drakina would be the one to do it.

Every moment counted.

CHAPTER FIVE

K raw, viceroy of Incendium, awakened with the sudden conviction that he was no longer alone.

Yet it was the middle of the night.

In a way, it was a relief. He had expected this ever since the return of the crown princess Drakina, and he preferred to face his terrors rather than have nightmares of dread.

He rolled over in his bed, glanced at the doorway and his heart sank. The princess Drakina was silhouetted there, but worse, sparks ignited at the ends of her long red hair.

Though no door in the palace was closed to the imperial family, Drakina showed her father's courtesy and waited on the threshold to be invited into the viceroy's apartment.

Kraw sat up and tried to look suitably dignified to greet her, but doubted his own success. His nightshirt was rumpled, for his sleep had been restless, and he was certain his mustache—the pride of his days—was at less than its best. He had finally fallen asleep on the couch in the formal room instead of his bedroom. While this meant he could see the princess easily, it also posed some challenge to receiving her in the appropriate manner.

Still, there was no denying the royal will, or presence.

Kraw cleared his throat. "My grandfather wrote in his chronicles that when you were irked as a child, your hair turned to flame," he dared to say.

The princess, to his relief, laughed a little. "You don't remember?"

"Of course not, Highness. You were a wyvern fully grown by the time I was born." He rose from the couch, bowed, then turned on the lights. He gestured to the seating area by the window and the princess inclined her head with grace before entering his home. He hurried to don a robe of brocade, hoping it was sufficiently fine for her view, but knew there was no time to dress properly. "May I offer you refreshment, Highness?"

Drakina smiled as she took a seat. "I don't expect such courtesy, Kraw. In fact, I owe you an apology for troubling you at this hour."

"I am certain you had cause, Highness."

Drakina looked him up and down, her slow survey making Kraw keenly aware of the flaws of his appearance. But then she smiled at him, and there was sympathy in her expression. "I would never have done it, Kraw," she admitted softly. "No matter how vexed I was, but I had a sense that you might be as sleepless as I, and for a similar reason."

Kraw's knees nearly gave out beneath his weight. The moment he had feared had arrived, and he felt that curious mingling of terror and relief. He didn't believe that the princess would welcome the truth. This might prove to be his last night in the service of the royal family of Incendium. On the other hand, the secret had weighed heavily upon him, and he would be glad to surrender it—no matter what the price.

"You look as if you should sit down, Kraw," she said gently.

"Not in the royal presence, Highness..."

Drakina stood up, turned a chair, and gave Kraw's shoulder a firm push. He sat down, then sighed with relief.

She sat down opposite him and fixed him with a look. "You planned it all." There was no question in her tone. "Why, Kraw? Why?"

"I did not plan it all, Highness. I tried to serve your family in the tradition of mine..."

She raised a hand for silence. "Just tell me, please, what happened."

Kraw studied her, discomfited that he could no longer guess her thoughts. The sparks had died, which was encouraging, but there was a solemnity about her that he did not associate with the princess Drakina. He licked his lips. "Did you..."

"I have conceived the crown prince, Kraw," she said, interrupting him. Her hand stole over her belly. "The egg will hatch in the summer. My father is pleased."

Kraw exhaled, glad that one hurdle had been cleared.

"Tell me of the Terran," she urged. "The MindBender." She smiled a little. "The greatest MindBender in the galaxy. Why exactly was he supposed to kill me?"

The viceroy's gaze flew to that of the princess, and he realized that she already knew much of the story. He sighed and frowned. "It was a wager, of the kind that they make on Xanto over the fates of the condemned. It says little good of the gamblers, to my thinking, that they sport with the lives of these creatures, making wagers and posing challenges, giving the condemned hope of survival if they can succeed at some ridiculous feat, then betting upon their success. It is barbaric. But when the MindBender was condemned to be executed, I understand there were many such proposals made to the Xantonians. They accepted the one that amused them most."

"That the MindBender could live if he killed me."

Kraw nodded.

"Whose proposal was it?"

"You must know, Highness, that there are those who did not agree with the ruling of the tribunal in the fate of Prince Canto..."

"I have heard a name already," she said then stood up and paced the width of the room and back. "Tell me, Kraw. I would know the worst."

Kraw winced. If she had heard the tale from the MindBender himself—and who else could have shared it?—then she knew the worst of it. "I have been warned against the crown prince, Urbanus."

"Gemma's fiancé," Drakina said, as if he did not know.

"But there is no evidence, Highness." Kraw took a steadying breath. "Your father chooses not to indulge in rumor, and the last time Queen Arcana was challenged, the furor was difficult to calm."

"He is known to enjoy his pleasures, Kraw, and to be extravagant."

"That might put him in the company of those gambler on Xanto but does not prove his involvement."

The princess fixed him with a glare. "The Carrier named him."

"Ah." Kraw rubbed his brow, knowing she would not like what he said next. "Incendium law code forbids the inclusion of testimony from a condemned man, be he citizen or nay."

The princess pursed her lips and looked out the window. "Continue, please."

"I heard the rumor, your father dismissed it and forbade action upon it. Truly, I would not have thought it possible for such a quest to succeed so consoled myself that the situation was not dire." Kraw sighed. "Until one of the astrologers divined the identity of your destined mate."

"Troy, the MindBender."

"Yes. A MindBender, a convict hired to assassinate you *and* a Terran. Truly, Highness, I did not know which was the worst of his credentials!"

Drakina watched him closely, and Kraw did not doubt that she saw all of the anguish he had experienced. "Did you tell my father?"

The viceroy bowed his head. "Only that he was the Carrier. Forgive me, Highness."

"You could have warned *me*."

"No, not with your father so set against Terrans and you so determined not to wed. I had to contrive a situation in which you might conceive the crown prince. I would have arranged for an escort for you, Highness, to ensure your protection."

Drakina smiled. "But I declined them, just as I defeated Urbanus' plan." Her gaze was shrewd. "Is there more for you to confess?"

The viceroy swallowed. "I cannot speak of it, Highness."

She held his gaze, then nodded once. "And what will happen to Troy? The MindBender?"

"He has been returned to Xanto and will be executed." Kraw's tone softened. "He accepted the wager, but he lost, Highness. He did not kill you." He rubbed his brow. "I suppose this spares your father the unpleasant task of denying the Carrier a role as your Consort."

Drakina stood silently at the window, and Kraw wondered what claimed her attention. The city was alight, as always it was, and the starport gleamed high overhead. He could see a shuttle descending, but knew her vision was more keen than his own. She rubbed her belly absently, her hand tracing little circles upon it, and he had never seen her so thoughtful.

"Troy lost on purpose, Kraw," she admitted finally. "Because he loved me." Her voice softened and fell low. "He asked me to tell our son something good about him." She paused again. "I believe Troy is my HeartKeeper."

Kraw knew he had to ask the unwelcome question. "Are you certain, Highness? It would not be unusual for a MindBender to mislead..."

Drakina spun to face him, conviction in her pose and her tone. "I *know* it, Kraw," she said. "Just as I know that I love him in return. I had to consider whether the tumult I felt was a fleeting passion, but every moment we are apart, convinces me that I love him. I don't want to live without Troy, Kraw. I will not let him be executed, and I will not let Urbanus remain unscathed in this. I need your help."

"I would be honored to be of any assistance, Highness."

"When will they kill him?"

Kraw winced. "It will not be long, Highness. Justice is quick in Xanto and I believe there have been payments made..."

"But it is not justice, Kraw." She flung a computer wafer at him, and he caught it. He realized it was loaded with precedents and galactic law codes. "He was a slave. He was seized from a planet we are supposed to defend from knowledge, sold illegally on the shadow market to the Gloria Furora, and tortured when he refused their commands. No court should have condemned him."

"Highness! I had no awareness..."

"No one did, Kraw. I expect a great many credits changed hands to see this done. No one wanted to remember who ordered that Arista be killed."

Arista! Kraw was glad that he was sitting down. His thoughts flew as he recalled the details and Gemma's fury at the death of her friend.

Then he thought of practicalities. "Highness, if this is to be done, we shall need a legal opinion compiled and a formal appeal..."

"I know you will arrange it all, Kraw." She leaned closer, her eyes glittering. "My HeartKeeper has been shown many injustices, and I will see them righted."

"Of course, Highness, though we must begin immediately. You have done much of the labor, but the argument should be dispatched by second light at the latest..." The viceroy fell silent in his planning as Drakina caught his face in her hands.

Much to his astonishment, she kissed him quickly, her gratitude and impulsiveness bringing tears to his eyes. "Thank you, Kraw!" Then she swept to the door. "In the meantime, I am going to Xanto, to claim my Consort."

"Wait! Highness! Your father will not accept a Terran in his court."

Drakina's eyes flashed green fire. "My father will accept my Consort as the father of his heir, or we shall abandon Incendium together and take the boy with us." She took tall and looked formidable. "Truly, my father is the least of the obstacles before us."

Kraw bowed to disguise his smile of delight. If anyone in the court could change the mind of King Ouros, it was Drakina, and in this matter, he believed she was right. "I understand, Highness."

"Would you be so kind, Kraw, as to help with the arrangements? I would like to leave as soon as possible, and this time, I *will* take an entourage."

"Perhaps a diplomat or two, Highness?"

Drakina laughed. "A good half dozen diplomats, Kraw, if you please. I know my weaknesses."

She was gone then, leaving Kraw with an enormous list to complete. He dressed in haste, summoned his seven most promising attendants, and launched into the most hectic day in all his memory.

But this, this was the service Kraw loved to

provide to his patron and king. Justice would be served, thanks to the intervention of Incendium, and King Ouros would receive all the credit.

Kraw's grandfather would have been proud.

And so it came to this.

Troy had never imagined he'd end his days in a penal colony in a far corner of the galaxy, nor did he imagine that he'd be executed for using his skills as commanded. But there was no doubting the purpose of the black chair on the pedestal before him.

He'd been roused at first light, had washed and shaved. He was naked, the better to ensure that he couldn't hide any surprises from his captors, but he walked tall between his two jailors. His mind was numb, for he had been drugged to ensure that he couldn't MindBend anyone in his vicinity.

His heart ached.

A crowd had gathered to watch his execution, and he was surprised by their numbers. He wasn't surprised by their obvious anticipation. There was nothing like an execution to bring out the worst in every kind. The procedure had been explained to him, and he doubted there'd be much drama. Not enough to justify their gathering, but bloodthirst wouldn't be denied.

There was no hope of a reprieve. No one in all of the galaxy wanted Troy alive enough to challenge his execution.

It wasn't a surprise, but it was a disappointment.

On Xanto, prisoners were executed by lethal injection. Troy would be strapped into the chair, made helpless, and the toxin, which had been precisely calibrated to his species and metabolism, would be injected into his arm. He'd feel as if he were falling asleep, but he wouldn't wake up ever again.

It would take less than four heartbeats. He'd been told as much and he believed it.

Troy saw his old employer in the audience, as well as an assortment of familiar gamblers. Prince Urbanus who had set the wager against Drakina was there, and Troy wondered whether he knew that Drakina had conceived. He hoped that she managed to defend herself against future attacks, because he was pretty sure there would be some.

Troy wished he could have survived to defend her himself, but that hadn't been an option.

The stone was cold beneath his feet, the penal colony of Xanto seeming even less hospitable on this cold and rainy morning. He could hear that the mines were silent, the work having been stopped so that the other inmates could witness his death.

Troy was to be a lesson for them.

In the days since his retrieval, he had been angry and he had been bitter. He had petitioned for appeal, based on Drakina's arguments, but every request had been denied. He might still have been feeling the weight of the injustice done to him, but the drug that suppressed his MindBending powers left him despondent. Fatalistic. What would be would be.

There was no point in fighting. He was vastly outnumbered and without his one gift, he wouldn't get far. He sat down in the chair and caught his breath at the chill of it against his thighs. But then, he wouldn't be cold for long.

Troy found himself thinking of that hunt with Drakina, the way she'd raced after the boar. It had felt to him like a wild and reckless ride, but she'd been completely in control. He smiled, remembering the wind in his hair, the exhilarating sense of her power, the connection he'd felt with her that day. He was glad, despite the ending to his own story, that he'd taken Urbanus' offer and had met her.

She'd changed his life, thawed his heart, convinced him to love.

Maybe they had been destined to mate.

Maybe she *would* tell the kid something good about him.

Troy's ankles had been shackled as well as his wrists. His jailors tightened the strap that bound his chest to the chair. This was it. The end. He found his heart racing, even though he knew that would only make the poison work faster.

They were about to blindfold him when there was a blinding flash of light.

Troy laughed aloud at the glorious sight of his Drakina. She appeared in front of him, not in the gallery for the audience. Her hair was loose and flowed around her as if it was alive. The tips lit with flames and she seemed to be throwing sparks into the air. She wore a dress of orange and red, one that flowed over her curves and could have been made of flame. It was feminine and sexy, but there was no hiding the sheer power of her body. Her eyes were glittering green, her lips curved in a satisfied smile.

Trust Drakina to transport right into the middle of an execution. He knew the location had been precisely calculated for maximum effect.

Troy was reminded of her entry into MacEnroe's Pub and knew that she liked making an entrance. This time, she had an entourage, many of them as richly garbed as she was, probably thirty attendants who had transported with her. What an expense! Troy was impressed that they had appeared in rank and with minimal disarray. The audience stirred in interest that they would get a show after all.

Drakina met his gaze and blew him a kiss, then turned to challenge the Emperor of Xanto. "You will not execute the Consort of the crown princess of Incendium," she declared, her voice carrying over the audience. "You will immediately surrender my destined mate to my custody." There was a protest, of course, but Drakina raised her voice. "His trial was so unfair that it seems likely the verdict was bought."

There was a bustle amongst the judiciary and the Emperor began to rise to his feet.

Drakina raised her voice. "I have brought an auditor from the Interstellar Office of Accounts to review the transactions recorded on the books of the court," Drakina continued smoothly. "The better to ensure that there is neither inconvenience or delay."

The Emperor's eyes narrowed. The comments became louder in the gallery, but Drakina ignored them. She gestured and four of her attendants hastened forward with the official argument. Although it could have been summarized on a tiny computer sheet, Troy guessed that Drakina had brought it on scrolls for effect.

There were a lot of scrolls. "I also have brought the appeal, brought by the King of Incendium on behalf of the prisoner, and all of the supporting arguments in its favor. I would be happy to second these lawyers to the Emperor's court for the duration of the appeal."

"This is quite sufficient," the Emperor declared, obviously trying to regain control of the situation, but Drakina continued as if he had not spoken.

If anything, her voice became louder. "The prisoner, as my Consort, will be taken into the custody of the court of Incendium, for his own protection."

"I protest!" declared the Emperor.

"Because you would sell his fate again?" Drakina demanded in a booming voice. A large percentage of the spectators quailed. She pointed at the governor of Xanto. "It is an outrage that such games are tolerated in a universe said to be civilized." She gestured and seven clerks stepped forward. "Here is the case brought against the Governor of Xanto by the Kingdom of Incendium for the violation of fundamental rights due to all sentient beings."

"But..." protested the emperor's aid.

"And here are the charges against the Pirates of Manganus Five, for seizing a Terran in violation of interstellar code," Drakina continued, beckoning to another four clerks bearing scrolls. She folded her arms across her chest. "I leave the Gloria Furora to you, for the moment." She inclined her head at some beings in the crowd. "There was not sufficient time to delve into the labyrinthine tunnels of their affairs."

The emperor might have protested, but Drakina threw out her arms and shifted shape in a blaze of golden light. Her dragon form glittered and she breathed fire at the sky, then at the podium of dignitaries. The emperor stumbled backward, his robes aflame, and Troy heard cries of consternation.

He also saw Prince Urbanus scowl, then pivot and disappear into the crowd of spectators.

Drakina was either unafraid of the prince of Regalia or had another plan for him. Troy trusted her to have planned for every detail.

She turned a sparkling glance upon him, cutting through the drug's haze with one look. With one slash of her talons, he was cut free, then she snatched him in her talons and took flight. She soared over the dark mines of Xanto in triumph, holding him close against the thunder of her heart. "I like you naked, Carrier," she murmured, her tone teasing. "Maybe I will keep you this way."

"Maybe I'll make it worth your while, princess."

She landed with grace, shifting shape so that they stood together on the stone path he had just walked alone. One of the courtiers from Incendium cast a fur-lined cloak over his shoulders and another stood before them with a small volume.

"Marry me, Carrier?" Drakina asked, her gaze locking with his.

His heart raced, but he wanted her love, not her compassion. "Not for pity, princess."

Her eyes gleamed with resolve. "I know little of this pity," she said but he knew it wasn't true. She reached to touch his cheek, tentative. "I have mated with a warrior and would keep him as my Consort."

It was everything Troy had always wanted and more. He bent and kissed her thoroughly, vaguely aware the the official in front of them was clucking that the vows hadn't been exchanged yet. Many of those in the gallery shared his feelings, because they were cheering.

Troy felt like cheering himself. There was someone in the galaxy who wanted him alive, after all.

The official cleared his throat. "The vows, Highness?"

"Yes, the vows." Drakina gestured to another minion. "And please stream the ceremony to my father's court. By the time we return to Incendium, he may have made his peace with my choice." She cast a sparkling glance at Troy. "He will have a grandson to spoil, after all."

"When do you plan to go back?"

"After a seclusion as befits a couple newly bound." Her eyes twinkled. "I have been thinking of that boar, and that it should not go to waste."

Troy grinned. "It would be about time to smoke it, and roast a haunch."

Drakina's hand closed over his own. "And we will bring some of this bacon when we return to Incendium. It may be of aid in winning my father's agreement."

"That's brilliant, princess."

"We have conquered with teamwork before, Troy, and we will do so again and again." Her smile was confident and the weight of her hand in his was perfect. They turned to the official and exchanged their vows in clear voices.

For the first time, in a very long time, Troy felt optimism about his future.

No. He felt exhilaration about his future.

Because a dragon princess had claimed him for her own.

"This exchange of vows," Drakina said when the official stepped back. "Must be sealed with a kiss."

"You won't get an argument from me, princess."

The royal egg was delivered a little later than might have been expected, but Ignita assured Drakina—and Troy, who had been banished from the imperial birthing chamber—that this was normal for a first-spawn. The queen had been with her oldest daughter for the entire duration of the labor.

"You took much longer, Drakina," Ignita said with a laugh, her gaze lingering on the newly delivered egg. Drakina's sisters were in the nursery with her and her mother, along with the physician, six nursemaids, and a cluster of astrologers. It was an ornate and cozy room, without windows to ensure its security and better regulate its temperature, and generously proportioned for a reason.

The delivery of a royal egg always commanded a crowd.

The viewing of the royal egg before it hatched was also a popular activity.

It was not uncommon for a mother to unwillingly shift to her dragon form in the act of birthing the egg, which was yet another reason to have such a large room. Drakina was glad she hadn't done that, and that her mother had managed to restrain herself, as well.

She lay on a bed against one wall of the chamber. The egg was perched in the very middle of the room, at the focal point as it should be. Drakina thought it was the most beautiful dragon egg she'd ever seen. It was blue-green and shone with iridescence. The shell's surface was marked with opalescent patterns and caught the light. The physician bent over it, murmuring and listening as everyone else watched him in rapt silence. There was a tension in the chamber until his features brightened.

"The crown prince quickens!" he declared and there were tears of joy, as well as shouts of delight. Drakina's sisters kissed her one after the other, and her mother began to sing.

Even in the sheltered room, Drakina could hear the bells pealing in the city below, informing the citizens of Incendium of the good news. There would be feasting on this night, courtesy of King Ouros. It had been a long time since Peri's delivery, but memories ran long in Incendium of the lavish spreads bestowed on the populace when an egg quickened.

There was more to celebrate as well, for Troy had been officially pardoned. Just the day before, he'd received an official apology from the Emperor and another from the Governor of Xanto.

The locked portals to the chamber were opened, and Troy was summoned. The egg was surrounded by nursemaids who wrapped it in ermine and silk and tucked it into a warm nest. The astrologers hovered at the perimeter of the chamber, desperate to begin their examination of the shell's surface and chart the horoscope of the crown prince, but they had to wait.

Troy was the first male through the doors, but he came directly to Drakina instead of the egg. Gemma was beside Drakina and she momentarily blocked

Troy's path. It might have looked inadvertent to another, but both Drakina and Troy knew better. Drakina knew the hard shimmer in her sister's eyes was enough to freeze the blood of many men.

Troy bowed and excused himself.

"I may never excuse you," Gemma said tightly, then moved out of his path.

Troy paused to hold her gaze, so unafraid that Drakina was proud. "Remember that I have been an assassin. If there is a man you would seek to kill, Gemma, I might be of aid to you."

"I do not need your aid," she replied, her voice hard.

"I can stand testimony against Urbanus now."

Gemma lifted her chin. "I will solve this matter myself."

Troy's gaze was simmering when he bent to kiss Drakina's cheek. "All right, princess?" he murmured for her ears alone.

"Never better," she said, and kissed him properly.

Gemma averted her face but didn't leave.

When Troy went to look at the egg, Drakina appealed to her sister yet again. "You should break the betrothal, Gemma," she advised quietly. "You should not marry Urbanus."

Meanwhile, Gemma smiled, a warrior princess to her toes. She was blond with blue eyes, and often underestimated for her prettiness. When her dragon was ascendant, though, it was impossible to imagine she was anything else. "I will keep the betrothal, and I will wreak vengeance from inside his own home. Nowhere is it writ that I will welcome him as my wedded husband." She arched a brow. "Urbanus will know the fullness of my wrath only when it is too late for him to save himself."

"Then you do not need Troy's help."

"I do not."

"But if Urbanus guesses..."

Gemma laughed. "Does he come to the quickening? No. He and his mother are casting spells, I am sure." She shook her head. "As if words could save him."

Drakina frowned. "Don't imperil yourself, Gemma. Vengeance is not noble."

"But sometimes it is necessary," she said with heat then walked away.

Drakina watched as Troy walked around the egg, his expression a mix of wonder and curiosity. Ouros was close behind him—and he examined the egg first— his pleasure with events more than clear.

Ouros even spoke to Troy, which was progress. Drakina guessed that her father was explaining the marvel of this particular dragon egg and how it exceeded all others.

Mostly because it contained his first grandson.

Troy glanced at Drakina and their gazes met, his slow smile prompting her lips to curve in return.

"Kraw!" Ignita called. "We must make ready for the blessings!"

"Indeed, Highness, the tidings have journeyed quickly. The High Priestess of Nimue has already arrived to give her blessing."

Drakina saw Troy wince at the news of their visitor. How did he know the High Priestess? Or what did he know of her?

Ignita fluttered, then hurried from the chamber to ensure that all was made ready for her guests. Gemma joined Ignita at the portal to welcome the first of those come to bless the egg.

Troy came to Drakina's side and perched on the side of the bed. He took her hand and laced their fingers together. "I'd rather face the high court of Xanto than your sister," he murmured.

She nodded rueful agreement. "She has the longest memory and the strongest battle skills."

Troy grimaced. "There are more reassuring things you could have said."

"I meant that if there is anyone to avenge the crime of Regalia, it will be Gemma," Drakina clarified. "She will accept that you were not truly responsible for Arista's death, in time."

"I don't have your lifespan to wait, princess."

"That is something we must discuss," Drakina said, holding fast to his hand. "But you know I will protect you."

He surveyed her warmly. "And you are okay?"

"It was not so bad. I am glad that there is a quickening already." She spoke quietly to him, as the others hastened about.

"Were you afraid?"

"Concerned," she admitted with a smile. She patted the pillow and he lounged beside her, his long legs stretched out beside hers.

"Me, too," he replied and kissed her knuckles. "It's so strange that you revere astrologers over astronomers. That's not the way it is on Terra."

"It is so strange that you divide the knowledge of the stars, calling part science and part myth. It is all wisdom."

Troy nodded understanding, and she knew he was thinking of something else. "How long until he's born?" He frowned. "Or hatched?"

"Several months in your time, but he will be tended at every moment. The greatest peril is past." She squeezed his fingers and tried to encourage his confidence. "I hear that you have been down in the shipyards again."

"It's fascinating. I always liked engines, and the stellar drive is so interesting."

Drakina smiled. "It is said that you have offered good suggestions."

Troy grinned. "I've just asked questions, princess. There's so much to learn."

"Do you like it on Incendium?" she asked, fearing his response. Troy did not have to have an ongoing role in the court, not now that the crown prince was hale.

"I do. I think of Terra, sometimes, but I feel as if I have two homes."

"I am glad."

He turned to face her. "But I have an idea, princess. I haven't done any MindBending as it seemed it would be rude, but I've noticed something that you might not have seen."

"Tell me."

"Everyone in Incendium worries about the planet falling toward the sun."

"Surely this is reasonable."

"Of course, but what if that, if all those thoughts, are actually drawing the planet toward the sun? What if the focus of so many minds is accelerating

Incendium's fall?"

Drakina straightened. She had never considered the possibility, but Troy knew more of the power of the mind than she. "Never mind my father's concern."

"Right. There's a dragon who can make things happen by force of will!"

"What do you suggest?"

"I'm thinking that maybe you and I should return to Terra, with our son. It would be a huge change for you and a concession, I know—"

"Not so much of a concession, Troy, to be with you in the paradise you call home."

He smiled, obviously pleased by her words. That he hadn't expected them meant she had to confess more, once he was done. "Maybe that's how our son will save Incendium."

"I don't understand."

"All those people and dragons will turn their thoughts from the sun to our son." He pointed, and she realized that Terra was in the opposite direction, far away from the central star of their system. In fact, Terra was nearly as far from their sun as it was possible to be in the galaxy.

"And you think it might draw Incendium away from its sun."

"I think it's worth a try, princess."

"The boy's name has been divined, Highness," Kraw said, clearing his throat at close proximity. "It is to be Gravitas."

Drakina laughed aloud, for the astrologers had confirmed Troy's suspicion.

He grinned at her. "Maybe there is something

about destiny being in a name."

"My father will be greatly pleased if my Consort invites him for a regular visit and offers him the chance to hunt verran again."

She watched as Troy considered that. "I could do it," he said. "It's quiet around the farm. I could MindBend whoever is in the vicinity when your family visits and hide their dragon forms."

"It is perfect!" Drakina threw her arms around him and kissed him with enthusiasm. "Not only are you the Carrier and my Consort, but you are my HeartKeeper, Troy." She saw a flicker of confusion in his eyes, mingled with hope. "I love you," she said, choosing the Terran phrasing and saw him smile. "And that means I have a gift for you."

He raised his brows. "There's more?"

Drakina held fast to his hands, for this was no joke. "My kind live many centuries, Troy, and though we mate with men, men do not live so long as that."

"I've wondered about that," he murmured.

"Our wise women considered this question for many generations, until they created a potion." Drakina beckoned and Kraw brought a chalice to her. She had never before seen the purple liquid or smelled it, but she knew what it was. "It is only offered to a HeartKeeper who is not a dragon shifter, and he or she has the right to refuse it."

"What happens if I drink it?"

"Your lifeline will be matched to mine. You will not survive long after my demise." She smiled. "And if I drink it as well, then my lifeline will be bound to yours."

He smiled a little, his expression making her

heart skip and her blood warm. "Giving destiny a little help, princess?"

"Something like that."

Troy took the cup from Kraw, holding her gaze as he drank half of its contents. Without a word, he handed it to Drakina and she liked that he knew her intention even without peering into her thoughts. She drained the chalice, handed it to Kraw, then welcomed Troy's kiss.

Someone was admitted to the chamber, and they broke their kiss with reluctance. Drakina was too busy holding Troy's gaze to be curious about the new arrival. She was thinking instead of how soon they might celebrate the delivery of the egg, and how soon they might return to Terra...then she realized his features were changing. Before her very eyes, his face shifted from the form she'd once found ugly to a splendidly handsome countenance. A different man, and yet the same one.

He looked like a king. A prince.

A man for whom a thousand ships might be launched.

"Troy?" she whispered, reaching with her fingertips to touch his jaw. "What is happening?"

"I didn't know the potion did *that*," Callida commented.

"It doesn't, Majesty," Kraw said.

Drakina frowned. "Then what is wrong? Why is this happening?"

Troy leapt to his feet, and peered into one of the mirrors on the walls of the chamber. Then he hooted with delight and returned to swing her in the air. "You broke the spell, princess," he declared and his joy was unmistakable.

"What spell?" Drakina asked. She was relieved that his mouth had not changed at all, though she liked that he was so pleased.

"As part of his punishment, the MindBender was condemned to look as he did," the High Priestess of Nimue declared. She was the one who had entered the chamber and stood by the portal in her robes that flowed like water, leaning upon her silver staff. A fiery gem glinted in the setting at the top of her staff, like a watchful eye in the night. One of her white snakes peered through a gap in her robes, revealing that it was coiled around her waist. It, too, had watchful eyes. "I saw in the future that love could save the MindBender from his execution, but the high judge of Xanto did not believe a dragon princess could love a man who looked like that." She smiled. "We made a little wager."

"Fiends!" Drakina declared.

"They stacked everything against me that they could," Troy muttered.

"Because they understand nothing about my kind," Drakina replied with fury. Even as she marveled at the change in Troy's appearance, she knew it made no difference to her feelings. The High Priestess looked between them with satisfaction, then crossed the room to bless the egg.

But Drakina cared only for Troy. No matter his appearance, his nature was the same. He was a warrior, a champion, and the man who had won her love.

"HeartKeeper," he repeated, his gaze dropping to her lips. "I definitely like that title best of all the ones you've given me, princess."

"And that is good," Drakina said, looping her arm around his neck to draw him closer. "For it is one you cannot abandon."

"Just try to take it from me, princess," he whispered, his eyes shining, then slanted his mouth over hers in a most satisfying kiss.

It was both slow and thorough, which suited Drakina very well.

NERO'S DREAM

The Dragons of Incendium 1.5

DEBORAH COOKE

CHAPTER ONE

N ero had to pinch himself.

Again.

Not only had he survived the trek to the capital city of Incendium, not only was the city more of a glittering and bustling wonder than he'd ever imagined, not only was he inside the imperial palace—but he was to have a hearing with the viceroy, Kraw.

It was worth another pinch. To be standing in this antechamber with its floor inlaid in a geometric pattern of stones, its vaulted ceiling showing the coats of arms of every territory in Incendium, was beyond his wildest aspirations.

He wasn't surprised though. He'd cast the chart for this day and been amazed by it. This was a day fraught with meaning. A day in which dreams could come true. A day in which secrets could be revealed, in which fortunes could be made, in which futures would be set. Nero had been over the chart again and again. He had checked his sources a hundred, no, a thousand times, and this day was one of the great nexus points.

A crossroads in the lifelines of many.

Including himself.

Nero didn't underestimate the potential of that.

He had dreamed all his life of visiting the capital city. He had imagined the marvel of entering the palace. Already two of his smaller hopes were achieved and it wasn't even midday. He might even catch a glimpse of one of the royal family on this day, and see a third goal achieved. The twelve princesses of Incendium were all dragon shifters, each more beautiful than the last. At the possibility of even being close to one of them, Nero had to take a deep breath and close his eyes. He'd studied the holograms. He'd seen them on the vid. He'd been enthralled by the princesses his entire life. Even being in the imperial palace—where they must also be—made his very marrow quiver.

If one spoke to him, he might not survive the encounter. His heart might explode.

The dragon shifters ruled Incendium, both because they were aristocrats and because they lived much longer than mortal men. In eons past, they had possessed the time to build their power, and to defend it. They mated rarely, typically with men or women as this was believed to protect the integrity of their lineage. The child was always a dragon shifter.

Rare was the union between two dragon shifters, such as that between the current king and queen. There were those—including Nero—who believed that was the reason for the prosperity of Incendium since that wedding day. Fortune smiled upon the kingdom. The horoscopes were radiant with opportunity and wealth.

Except for this day, which appeared as a shadow on Nero's chart.

A blot on the proverbial sun.

The astrologers in the royal court divined the destined mates of each imperial dragon and Nero couldn't believe that they had endorsed the marriage between Canto and Drakina. They were not destined mates. Canto could not be Drakina's HeartKeeper.

Why had anyone even tried to arrange such a dynastic match?

Even without the chart, Nero would have guessed the pairing to be ill-fated.

And now he brought the proof of it to the royal court. In proving his abilities, he might achieve his dream of becoming an astrologer in the royal court. It could happen on this day, as a result of this portent he delivered. It was within his grasp.

Maybe then he'd get used to seeing the princesses.

Maybe he'd manage one day to speak to one.

He turned the scroll in his hands, his palms damp. But first hurdles first. The imperial city was a long way from the quiet town of Mola where Nero had grown up, but his prophecy couldn't have been entrusted to a courier.

He had to deliver it himself, to Kraw.

Here he stood, still in his dusty traveling cloak and his muddy boots. He needed a shave and probably a haircut, and was not fit to see the imperial majesties, but he could not have delayed the delivery of the prophecy. It was too important. Time was too pressing.

Nero knew his prediction would be unwelcome. The entire city was aflutter with preparations for the royal wedding and to hear that the nuptials were not destined to occur would not be good news.

He wondered yet again why the royal astrologers hadn't seen this truth.

He wondered if they had but no one had mentioned it outside the palace.

Maybe no one had believed it.

Why had the match been arranged?

Myriad shuttles were descending from the starport, bringing guests from allies and other worlds. Nero had seen the shuttles gleaming in the distance, even two days before as he walked toward the city, and still more came. There were decorations in the streets and the day itself had been declared a holiday. He'd seen families walking toward the imperial gates, hoping to catch a glimpse of the happy couple after they exchanged their vows. He'd had to come through the kitchen entrance—no less busy, given the number of tradesmen delivering food for the feast to follow the service—and had been told twice that Kraw had no time for such folly as a message from one such as he. Only Nero's insistence and his persistence had gotten him this far.

He was right and he knew it. Sapior had taught him well.

A clerk in the livery of Regalia had arrived just before Nero and had been ushered up the stairs immediately, while Nero had been shown to this room.

It *had* been a long time since he'd been left here.

Nero feared suddenly that they had placed him in

a corner of the palace to be forgotten since he wouldn't go away. He checked the door, only to discover that it was secured from the other side. His prophecy must be heard, as soon as possible! He spun in the middle of the chamber, seeking another way out, but there was none.

He drew his knife, determined to force the lock on the door. He had no sooner laid his hand upon the latch than the door opened silently.

To reveal a dignified older man on the threshold, with a magnificent white moustache dressed in the livery of the king.

He had a gaze cold enough to strike terror into a dragon shifter.

In fact, Nero would have bet that this man had perceived at least three of his secrets, and all of his hopes and dreams. That with just a glance.

He looked Nero up and down again, then met the younger man's gaze. "You are the one who calls himself an astrologer?" His skepticism was clear.

Nero had expected that. He hadn't attended the Royal University of Astrologers. But that didn't mean Sapior's teachings were wrong.

Even if they were unconventional. Sapior had attended the university, made a discovery and been cast out for daring to suggest the ancient methods could be improved.

It occurred to Nero in that moment just how the royal astrologers might have missed the truth.

"Yes, sir, I am." Nero bowed low. "I come to offer what I have learned, in service to my lord king."

The older man frowned. "I am Kraw, viceroy of

Incendium. I do not have time this day for whimsy, young man. If this is a jest, you will regret it."

"I understand, sir, but it is neither whimsy nor a jest. I bring a dire prophecy."

Kraw arched a brow.

Nero unfurled the scroll he had carried all the way from Mola. "I can show you, sir, how the stars aligned in this horoscope..."

"The prophecy," Kraw interrupted crisply.

Nero closed his mouth and met the viceroy's gaze squarely. "The princess Drakina and the prince Cantos will not be wed this day. Ensuing events will cause a furor between the royal houses of Incendium and Regalia, if not an outright crisis."

"Why?"

"Because the crown prince Canto will die."

Kraw smiled thinly. "I fear you are mistaken."

"Sir! If you'll just look..."

Kraw's eyes narrowed and he backed out of the doorway. "The wedding ceremony will begin within moments. The family is already assembled. Your prophecy is wrong. I thank you for your concern on behalf of the royal family, but you are mistaken."

"I'm right! If you'll just look!"

Kraw's tone became steely. "You have made a mistake, as inexperienced astrologers often do. You have no place here and will immediately be escorted to the gates." He stepped back and snapped his fingers, which brought an armed man to his side.

Nero couldn't believe it. He hadn't come this far to be turned aside. He'd never even imagined that he wouldn't be able to deliver the prophecy. He'd expected to be doubted, but not silenced.

Outrage made him bold. Nero stepped forward, making the only gamble he could. "Sir! If I could show one of the royal astrologers..."

"You cannot." Kraw lowered his voice and spoke more kindly. "I am certain your intentions are good, but this is a day of relentless demand. Travel safely back to wherever you are from." The viceroy pivoted and was immediately surrounded by half a dozen servants seeking his counsel on one matter or another.

How could Nero warn them if they wouldn't listen?

How could he stand witness to a travesty he could have helped them to avoid?

"You can't linger," the guard warned him and gestured toward the corridor that led from the antechamber to a minor door. "Hurry along."

Nero hadn't taken three steps when he heard processional music echoing through the palace. The wedding was beginning!

The guard urged Nero toward the door. "Come on. I'm supposed to be upstairs already." When Nero hesitated, the guard dropped his hand to the hilt of his knife. "Don't make trouble," he advised. "Not today. Think of the princess. It's her wedding day."

Nero did think of the princess and felt compassion for her. He allowed himself to be ushered out of the palace, although he wished he could think of a reason to do otherwise. He stood in the courtyard, letting people hurry around him and reviewed his cred. He had less than five units to his name. He knew without looking in his purse. He'd spent everything in making this journey, planning on at least a small reward and hoping for a position at court. He didn't even have enough to pay for a night in the meanest hovel.

He felt like a fool.

He'd better start walking back home. He'd find a quiet place outside of town, maybe a barn or a shed, use a little of his dreamweed and try to divine where he'd gone wrong.

Nero had turned to leave when he realized the music had stopped.

In fact, the palace had fallen strangely silent. Everyone might have been holding their breath at once.

What had happened?

Was it the prophecy?

Nero heard the clatter of running footsteps and a man burst out of the same door he had just left. It was the clerk from Regalia, but now he looked terrified. He shoved Nero out of the way and ran for the gates, as if his worst nightmare was fast behind him. Nero lost sight on him en route to the star station.

There was a scream from inside the palace, a scream that made everyone in the courtyard cower in fear.

A dragon scream of rage.

There was a crash of breaking glass, and Nero realized in horror that the roof of the palace had been smashed. Still, his heart thrilled at the sight. A dragon of deepest green, scales gleaming like obsidian, roared into the sky and breathed a plume of fire toward the stars. Such power! Such majesty!

It was the princess Drakina.

When the dragon princess pivoted in the air, her great black wings flapping leisurely, everyone in the imperial city watched in awe. She turned to scan the city below and Nero saw her gaze brighten. She dove downward, swooping low over the courtyard, clearing the gates, and reaching a talon down into the crowd. Her precision and grace were awesome, and he watched with wonder as she soared high again, claws empty. She circled, breathed fire, and spiraled toward the earth again.

Nero knew then that his prophecy had come true.

"Where is that astrologer?" Kraw bellowed. He raced back down the stairs from the ceremonial chamber, moving as quickly as he could through the press of people. Already he was envisioning war between the two planets, which was never more than a puff of smoke away. Disaster had to be averted.

If it wasn't already too late for that.

The viceroy was followed by a coterie of royal astrologers, more than one of them curious about this arrival and his tidings. There were already murmurs of the new arrival being a fraud—for none of them had discerned this dire portent, which meant it had to be wrong or a trick—and demands to see his calculations. He might even be responsible for these events! Astrum, the oldest and grumpiest, wished to know his assumptions, as well as his credentials.

Kraw wanted to know what else the arrival had divined. He was a man of remarkable appearance, simply dressed but bright of eye. Kraw had been certain of the power of his intellect, if not the merit of his conclusions. There was an air of mystery about the professed astrologer, which the viceroy instinctively distrusted.

Men of mystery were often unpredictable. They brought change and challenge, neither of which were welcome to Kraw.

He didn't fail to note this man already showed that tendency.

He found him in the courtyard, waiting with a dignity that Kraw found admirable despite himself. The viceroy paused to catch his breath, then proceeded toward the younger man.

"You were right," he acknowledged.

The barest smile touched the man's lips. He flicked a glance skyward. "So, I see."

"What did you see?"

The younger man unfurled his chart again and the astrologers of the court clustered around him. "That Prince Cantos would decline to wed Princess Drakina, that he would send a minion to the ceremony in his own stead, that Princess Drakina would take exception to this."

"And?" Kraw prompted.

He winced. "That she would retaliate."

"That none would be able to stop her," added the oldest astrologer, pointing to the new arrival's chart.

The astrologers winced and sighed as one. "And that there would be tumult between the two royal families as a result."

"How did you make these calculations?" Astrum

demanded, suspicion in his tone. "Our charts of the day look vastly different from this one."

"I was taught a method that reveals secrets more readily than traditional methods..."

"Who taught you?" Astrum boomed, but the viceroy pushed the astrologer aside.

"There is no time to compare technique," Kraw declared with an impatience he thought justifiable. "What is the princess Drakina going to do?"

The astrologers turned to the new arrival, letting him share the news.

"Whatever she does, sir, he doesn't survive it."

Kraw pinched the bridge of his nose and walked away, thinking furiously. He had thought this a poor match from the outset, not only because there was no sign that Cantos was the Carrier of the Seed, but because the natures of the betrothed pair were so different. It made no sense to him to arrange a dynastic match to ensure an alliance, knowing it would be barren.

But King Ouros was not to be defied.

It also didn't seem right to Kraw that a man would show such fear of his intended, even before the nuptials. It certainly wasn't fitting for a crown prince to cower. It *was* sensible to have a measure of caution when dealing with the royal family of Incendium, but showing fear, in Kraw's experience was a strategic error. There was not a predator in all of the galaxy that did not become more predatory when taunted with the scent of terror. It was in their very making.

And now, Cantos had insulted the dragon shifter he feared. In fact, he had insulted the entire house of

Incendium. Kraw doubted the matter would end well. He suspected, in fact, that it would end in a conflagration. The only possible advantage to the situation was that so many dignitaries and diplomats were gathered in the palace and had witnessed the insult. A tribunal might find justification in whatever actions were taken.

There were a thousand things to do to manage the situation, and only one individual Kraw could dispatch to do the most important one.

"You," he said, pointing at the newly arrived astrologer. "What is your name?"

"Nero, sir." He bowed, his manner expectant.

"Can you fly a Starpod?"

The would-be astrologer straightened and his eyes brightened. "I've flown the sim at the annual fair and won a prize."

The other astrologers chortled at this. "It is not the same," Astrum muttered, then reached for the chart. "Just as this is not the same as our calculations. I would review your findings."

The arrival flicked the chart out of Astrum's hands and rolled it again. "It is mine." Tension crackled between them.

"Where are you from?" Astrum demanded but Kraw silenced him with a gesture.

"Your sim experience will have to suffice," he said. "Go to the star station and take a Starpod. Tell them it is on my authority, if they ask. Follow the princess and try to stop her from doing anything rash."

The younger man looked skeptical, which Kraw took as another sign of his intelligence. "Is that possible, sir?"

"Probably not, but I expect a full report upon your return."

"Yes, sir. Thank you, sir."

There was an explosion from the star station and even from this distance, flames and smoke could be discerned. Kraw feared that was just the beginning. The green dragon soared into the sky again, carrying something.

Probably an injured clerk.

Kraw grimaced. "You had better hurry, Nero. Good luck."

The Starpod wasn't at all like the sim at the annual fair.

Nero had expected it to be newer and more sophisticated. He wasn't expecting it to be so radically different that it might have been a different vessel altogether. He supposed that Mola was a long way from the bright lights of the capital city.

There was a clear sphere in the middle of the dash, which appeared to float in its holder. At least that was familiar—even if it didn't have directions inscribed on it like the one at the fair. He considered the smooth control panel with something like horror, which the attendant took for awe.

What if he crashed it?

"Only the newest and the best for the imperial fleet," that man said. "Voice activated. You're going to love it." He patted the dash and it illuminated with a thousand pinpoints of light. "These babies rock." He grinned. "Of course, you'll need all the help you can get if you're going to catch Drakina."

With that, he was gone, the door sealed, and Nero strapped in. There was nothing on the dash that resembled the controls he knew.

Voice activated.

"Prepare for departure," he commanded, feeling a little silly talking to himself. The engine purred to life, which meant he wasn't actually talking to himself. "Mission is to pursue Princess Drakina," he said with more confidence. "Please request clearance from Incendium Control for lift-off and for departure trajectory." Glittering light surrounded the vehicle, which was a hundred times better than the sim.

Nero's heart was racing.

"You have right of way, Incendium six-five-nine," came a voice, which must have been from Incendium Control. "All pathways are cleared for you. At your leisure."

"At your leisure," repeated the ship.

Well, there was no reason to delay.

"Loose moorings. Power thrusters." Nero nodded as the ship followed his command. The station was crowded with vehicles, and he knew that he was being watched by others. Even the most junior mechanic probably had more flight experience than Nero did.

The princess was barely a speck in the sky.

"Lock coordinates on Princess Drakina," he commanded. The floating sphere illuminated and Nero closed his hand around it. He saw a crosshair of light appear on the inside of the windshield and rolled the ball until the crosshair locked on the silhouetted dragon. He tapped it when nothing happened and a light flashed.

"Coordinates set," the ship declared. "Departure imminent. Six, five, four…"

At zero, it rose from the landing pad, so smoothly and quietly that Nero wanted to applaud.

"Trajectory is verified to be clear," the ship continued. "All systems go."

Nero gripped the armrests, sensing that the ship waited on him. "Pursue," he declared and nearly laughed out loud when the ship shot through the air. He'd never felt or witnessed such acceleration and he had no doubt that there had been a sonic boom over Incendium behind him. If they'd made sims like this, every boy in Incendium would want to be a star pilot.

Instead of just most of them.

Best of all, Nero was closing on the princess, even though she had a head start.

Drakina flew high in the sky. He'd thought she intended to drop the clerk and let him die from impact, but maybe she meant for the poor man to suffocate. Nero's mouth went dry as he realized the perils of service in the vicinity of royal dragon shifters.

The price of being a messenger with bad tidings.

It was easy to see that he could find himself in the clerk's company.

Suddenly Drakina was surrounded by a clear sphere, and Nero knew that the stories about the abilities of the royal dragons to create a crystal orb were all true.

He also knew what she was going to do, right before she disappeared.

She only needed an orb if she was going to transport, and she could only use the orb to transport somewhere comparatively close.

Nero's mouth went dry when he guessed her destination.

Regalia.

The twin planet in this system.

The home of Prince Canto, the betrothed of Drakina.

She was going after him.

"Target is generating an orb," Nero informed the ship. "What destinations are in range?"

"There are three wormholes on the target's trajectory," the ship said. "The first..."

"Does one go to Regalia?" Nero demanded.

"Yes." The ship sounded a bit huffy, perhaps because it had been interrupted. "Only one of the three."

The orb shone and Nero knew it was complete. The princess, orb and clerk vanished from view. Only a wink of light flashed where they'd last been. Then it faded as well.

"Target has entered transport," the ship reported. "Please advise."

"Pursue," he commanded. "Use the wormhole to Regalia."

"Be advised that entering a wormhole so quickly after another vessel will result in turbulence," the ship said.

"Is it dangerous?"

"Various life forms find it uncomfortable or even painful. The ship's integrity will not be compromised."

"Pursue," Nero repeated, hoping it wasn't too awful. He didn't have time to wait for the turbulence to subside.

"Prepare for transport in ten seconds," the ship declared. "Ten, nine, eight..." The ship counted down as they shot even higher into the sky. Nero knew they had to be close to the point where Drakina had disappeared. He knew that the wormholes were mapped and hard to discern with the naked eye.

Suddenly, the Starpod shimmered, shuddered, and Nero's ears popped. A maelstrom swirled around the ship, obscuring the view. Even though he'd only ridden the sim, he knew this was the effect of the transport.

They had entered the wormhole.

The reality was much worse than the sim. He felt as if his skin had been turned inside out, his bones folded and his muscles stretched taut. His stomach heaved. Nero closed his eyes and said a prayer, wishing he'd been a little more diligent in his attendance of religious services.

Maybe he should have cast his own horoscope. At least then he'd know whether he would survive this adventure.

This day.

But no, Sapior had always warned against that.

A second later, the ship shimmered and shuddered again. The maelstrom swirled, looking more like spinning stars. Nero's skin was turned back the way he preferred it to be, his bones were unfolded and his muscles contracted to their usual dimensions. He willed his stomach to settle.

He was very glad—and intrigued—to see the forests of another planet beneath him. They were different from the forests he knew, but reassuringly like the vids he'd seen of Regalia. The tree branches glittered with a coating of hoarfrost, a chilly sight that made him shiver, even though he was warm inside the Starpod. The sun seemed fainter here and its light more cold. He had the strange feeling that he was being watched.

"Cruising altitude over Regalia, Frost Pole," the ship informed him. "Closing on target. Sixteen hundred seconds to rendezvous."

Nero could see the silhouette of Drakina far ahead of him. The crystal sphere popped and its shards scattered before they sparkled and disappeared. She was still in her dragon form and flew a circle around a turret perched on the top of a jagged peak. There was snow on the roof of the building, and the clouds that wreathed the peak made it look as if it towered high over Regalia. A pennant tugged at the top of the tower roof, and Nero saw it was emblazoned with the insignia of the royal house of Regalia.

A gold shield on a blue ground, with lances crossed behind it.

The dragon princess landed in the walled courtyard beside the tower, and Nero admired the accuracy of her landing. The ship was close enough for him to see that the man in her grasp *was* a clerk, because he was dressed in the livery of Regalia. She set him down in a courtyard with some care, and he ran for the portal without delay.

Did he flee her, or had she sent him to fetch the

crown prince? Nero saw Drakina settle back on her haunches, her eyes glowing as she apparently waited, and guessed the latter.

Then she turned her gaze upon him, her eyes narrowing as the Starpod landed beside her in the courtyard. "Target reached," the ship informed Nero. It then told him the coordinates of their location, the exterior temperature and wind direction, their proximity to the crown princess, and the amount of time he could remain and still have sufficient fuel to return to Incendium. It then opened the portal and wished him a pleasant day.

The way the princess was watching him left Nero skeptical of that possibility.

He hoped that dragons weren't as perceptive as they were rumored to be. He liked his secrets hidden.

But there was no question of returning to Incendium without tidings. The only way forward was through, and he'd come this far. Nero straightened his tabard, gripped the hilt of his very small knife, and left the ship with as much dignity as he could muster.

A flock of dark birds took flight suddenly, revealing that they had been nestled in the crenellations of the surrounding wall. They looked black against the cold sky, and were oddly silent. They flew away in a tight formation, and Nero had the sense that they had been summoned.

Or maybe they went to report what they had seen.

He shivered again. The princess Drakina smiled at the sight of him, and Nero stood tall before her, refusing to show any fear.

Chapter Two

Drakina didn't know him.

She would have remembered a man as beautiful as this. He was tall and muscled, broad shouldered and trim through the hips. His skin was as dark as ebony and his eyes the color of fine amber. She inhaled deeply, not really surprised to get a whiff of the grain fields of Medior, the gushing river at Mola, the seductive tinge of dreamweed.

He was from the equatorial zone of Incendium, or at least he had been there recently.

His clothing was simple but well made. He took care of his boots, and she could see that the ridiculously small blade he carried had been polished and honed. A thoughtful man, then, one who tended his responsibilities.

And one who was intrepid. He walked toward her, armed with only that small knife, wary but without hesitation.

She could have shifted shape to reassure him about her intentions, but Drakina wasn't in a mood to reassure anyone. Instead she lowered her head, her chin almost brushing the ground, so that their gazes were level.

He flinched, but only a dragon would have seen the fleeting reaction.

She was impressed.

"Sent to witness the carnage?" she asked, keeping her voice to a low rumble.

"I believe I was sent to *stop* the carnage, Highness," he said with a bow. He had a pleasing voice. Melodic. Deep. Drakina imagined he would sing well. There was a gleam in his eyes that made her think he was smarter than most. "But I know better."

"You know better than the command of my father?"

"It was the viceroy Kraw who sent me, Highness. I would not dare to challenge an edict from the king."

"Why do you think it can't be stopped?" Drakina was curious, despite herself. Fury simmered within her, but the faithlessness of Canto was not this man's fault.

He smiled ever so briefly, inclined his head as if to beg her forgiveness, then unfurled a scroll that he had been carrying on his back. She immediately saw that it was a horoscope. "If you see here, Highness, the death of Cantos at your talon is indicated in this quadrant of the chart..."

"You're an astrologer?" He didn't look like any of the royal astrologers. He was too young, too handsome...too charming.

"Yes, Highness. This chart and its portent brought me to the capital city, for I sought to warn your father..."

"But you didn't arrive in time?"

He opened his mouth, then closed it again.

Drakina smiled that he had some diplomacy. More than she did, at least. "You *did* arrive in time, but were not allowed to deliver your message."

"The viceroy was very busy with so many guests."

Drakina dropped her voice to a conspiratorial whisper. "I am glad. It would have been most awkward if my father had forbidden me to avenge the insult."

He looked discomfited with this.

"It is a question of honor," Drakina insisted. "And the insult to my father in his own home. It could not pass unchallenged, and it is better if I do the honors, so to speak."

"Of course, Highness." He fixed her with a look that was surprisingly courageous. "But you surely must understand that there will be repercussions."

"I should hope so! What kind of queen would let her son's death go unremarked?" Drakina straightened. "I expect a massive diplomatic incident. Maybe even war."

He was watching her. "But you guess that the inevitable tribunal will find in your favor."

"Will they?"

He nodded, proving that he was completely unlike the royal astrologers. They never gave straight answers, must less absolute ones.

"We need more astrologers like you at court," Drakina said. "Where are you from? Are there more like you?"

"Mola, Highness. A small town..."

"In Medior, where wizards are said to lurk in every shadow and all citizens partake of the pleasures of dreamweed."

"Not all, Highness."

Drakina waited.

"Children don't partake, for example."

She laughed but he cleared his throat.

"There are no more like me. My tutor Sapior taught me his methods before he died, for he had no child. I am the last to know his way of casting a horoscope."

"Was he self-taught?"

"He attended the university, Highness, but was cast out for his attempt to add an unconventional methodology to the curriculum."

Drakina considered the man who stood before her and hazarded a guess. "If his way requires the dreamweed, take care, Master Astrologer. My father has no tolerance of it, and any caught with it in their possession in his household are burned alive for the crime."

He bowed again, a little stiffness in his shoulders. He did use the dreamweed, then. "I thank you for your advice, Highness."

Before she could ask more, she became aware of the sharp tang of fear. She turned to eye the portal to the tower and discerned the clerk hiding in the shadows inside. He was pale still and she could see his knees trembling.

"Speak!" she commanded, letting her voice roar so that the stones rattled. Drakina could feel the clerk tremble and heard his heart skip a beat.

The astrologer, however, stood his ground and

watched avidly.

Fearlessly.

That would keep him alive in the palace.

"My lord prince declines to meet you, my lady," the clerk said, his voice faint.

"That is of no concern," Drakina said. "I will go to him."

The clerk squeaked, bowed, and raced up the stairs inside the tower. Drakina shifted shape, assuming her human form, and surveyed her wedding dress critically. The beads of gold and orange and red still shone brightly and the silk rustled as she moved. She looked at the astrologer.

"Magnificent, Highness." He bowed. "Your splendor rivals that of the sun."

She smiled. "You aren't afraid of me," she felt compelled to note.

His grin was quick and confident. He indicated the chart. "There is a witness indicated here in the margin, Highness. A man of little consequence, yet one who survives the encounter."

"You?"

"I hope so, Highness."

Drakina made for the door, knowing he would follow her. A witness.

She was no astrologer, but she had a that this man would not be considered to be of so little consequence after this day.

She strode into the tower, anger and purpose flooding through her. Canto would not share the happy fate of the astrologer from Medior.

Drakina was looking forward to ensuring that.

The stairs were steep and narrow, though the princess Drakina ascended them quickly. It was only as he hastened after her that Nero wondered whether they had been built that way in defense against dragons.

In her dragon form, the princess could never have climbed these stairs.

The fact that she could change shape at will meant they were no obstacle.

As a dragon, in fact, she could have torn the roof from the tower instead, and plucked out her reluctant suitor.

Perhaps the builders of Regalia did not think matters through.

The room at the top of the tower was of good size, but still not big enough for Drakina in her dragon form. It was simply furnished. Even from the stairs, Nero could see that there was only a curtained bed, a carved wooden chair, a table and an unlit brazier in the room. The shutters were open so that the room was filled with cold winter light, and the chill of the wind. A man sat on the bed, his face in shadows, his arms folded across his chest. He looked like a petulant child, not a warrior.

Not a king.

There was no barrier at the summit of the stairs, save the clerk.

"My lord prince is not receiving guests, my lady," he said.

"Canto will receive me," Drakina replied. "After all, I am no mere guest. I am his *betrothed*."

Even though Nero was behind the princess, he could feel the force of her will. He saw its effect upon the clerk, who took a step back.

"I have no wish to harm you," she said softly. "But no one will stand in my way on this day." She inhaled deeply, then dropped her voice even lower. "You must know that your terror makes you almost irresistible. It awakens my every urge to hunt."

The clerk's terror clearly doubled at that confession.

"Do not suffer her to pass!" cried the man on the bed.

The clerk looked between the two royals, his panic clear. He glanced at Nero, who had no intention of assaulting the princess on Canto's behalf. The prince remained where he was.

The clerk considered Drakina, his agitation rising. She took another step, and then another. He visibly trembled, then suddenly ducked to one side, covering his head with his hands.

Nero wondered what retaliation he expected that gave him the strength to resist for as long as he had.

The prince threw a crockery vessel at him. "Coward!" he shouted as it shattered against the stone wall.

"Coward?" Drakina swept into the chamber and crossed the floor to the bed. She shimmered a little in her fury, and Nero saw sparks flying from the ends of her hair. The crown prince made a little moan and eased to the back corner of the bed.

As if he would hide.

But that was impossible. Drakina seized the prince and threw him bodily on the floor. Evidently her strength was consistent between forms. Canto crawled backward, his horror clear, and her eyes flashed like lightning.

"Who is the coward, Canto? The servant who refuses to be a fool at his master's command, or the man who doesn't have the courage to speak for himself?"

"You know we'd never get along," Canto said hastily. "You know we couldn't make each other happy."

"Stand up and show your merit!" she commanded.

He got up with obvious reluctance, but didn't stand tall. He lifted his hands. "It won't work, Drakina..."

"So, you hid yourself away here and sent a minion to tell me of it." Drakina's scorn was clear. "You know that no king could endure the humiliation you visited upon my father's house this day!" She seized his shirt and lifted him to his toes with one hand. His eyes widened. "You could have made *one* protest in the year of our betrothal. You could have spoken to me. You could have arrived yourself to tell me."

Canto shook in her grip. "Drakina, I beg of you. Have mercy..."

"But you were a coward." Drakina's lip curled. "You sent a clerk."

"Drakina! Don't hurt me!"

"You joust," she reminded the prince with scorn. "You ride in tournaments. You're lauded for your bravery. How can this be?"

The prince flushed. "It's all arranged," he admitted, and Nero felt Drakina's disgust like a cold wave.

"Arranged? Your victories are bought?"

"Negotiated," Canto said. "And why not? I'm the crown prince."

"I cannot abide such timidity of spirit," Drakina seethed. Canto flailed in her grip but couldn't escape. "I thought you *valiant*. I thought you the gem in Regalia's crown. I thought I had to be wrong about you. Coward!"

"Liar!" he retorted, his face flushed.

Drakina stilled and her silence made Nero fear what she would do. "What is this?" she asked quietly.

"My mother guessed the truth, after the alliance was made," Canto said, growing more bold as he made his accusations. "She told me yesterday. You mean to destroy us all and make Regalia your own. You mean to populate it with the worms you bear and drive us out..."

"Worms?" Drakina echoed and put him on his feet.

Nero feared that was a bad sign, but Canto was emboldened by it. He straightened his shirt and his eyes flashed. "Yes, *worms*! The spawn of dragons," he spat. "Why should I wed a dragon? Why should my sons be dragons? Why should I participate in spreading the abomination of your kind? I can have any woman!"

Drakina smiled and examined her nails. "Our match would be barren, Canto," she said gently. "You need not fear such a fate, for yourself or your kingdom."

Canto took a step back. "Barren?" he repeated, his tone incredulous. "*Barren?*"

"You are not the Carrier of the Seed for me,"

Drakina explained mildly. "Our match seals a treaty, no more and no less." Her smile was chilly. "There will be no worms, as you call them. No eggs, either."

Canto was clearly shocked. "But my mother said..."

Drakina interrupted him crisply. "Queen Arcana would do well to abandon her grimoires for books of solid research. The biology of our kind is well documented. Any one of you could have learned the truth with very little effort. Must I add lazy to your list of attributes, Canto?"

"You lie!" Canto cried. "You want Regalia for your own! You will overrun us and steal all that is our own. This is no more than a trick, and I will not marry you."

"That would compromise the alliance between our kinds, the alliance to see our planets saved."

"You talk of science, but marriage has no effect on dying sons." Canto backed away from Drakina. "We can just part ways. No harm done."

"That is possible no longer," Drakina said sadly.

"We can be reasonable about this..."

"The time for reason is gone." She dropped her voice lower. "Consider, Canto, that if I take vengeance for my father, then he cannot take vengeance for me. It is the law."

Canto froze, new panic dawning in his eyes. "Vengeance?" he said, and his voice was a squeak.

Drakina's smile was cold. "You wanted me to show mercy, Canto."

His expression was wild. "But..."

"My father loves to hunt. He would welcome the opportunity to hunt you and extract a toll for what you did this day." She shook her head. "I doubt the payment would be rendered quickly."

The prince's face was white at this point and his lip trembled. He had backed into the wall.

Nero was intrigued. Drakina was clearly angry and insulted, but she didn't act solely out of passion. She *was* showing mercy.

Canto spared a glance at the window, as if he might flee.

"There is no escape, Canto. He can find you anywhere, just as I have done." Drakina strolled toward the prince. "Go ahead, Canto," she invited. "Beg me again to show you mercy."

He fell to his knees and seized the hem of her dress. He kissed it. "Just let me live, Drakina," he pleaded and his groveling made Nero wince. Drakina must have sensed his disgust for she turned to look at him. Nero had the strange sense that their thoughts were as one. "I'll never grant trouble to anyone again, Drakina. Just let me live."

Drakina arched a brow, inviting Nero's comment.

Nero cleared his throat. "You will live forever, my lord, in the memory of men, as a warning of the price of insulting the royal house of Incendium."

Canto gasped.

Drakina smiled. "I do like you, astrologer." she murmured with satisfaction. Canto dared to look up at her. "But not you," she said to the prince. "And now, it is time for mercy."

"Drakina!"

Her eyes shone as she seized Canto. She flung him bodily out the window, then leapt out the window herself. She shifted shape in a blaze of light, right after her foot left the sill. Nero raced to the window to watch.

Canto screamed as he tumbled toward the moat, far far below.

Nero saw Drakina in her dragon form sweep down to snatch the falling prince out of the air. She breathed a plume of fire into the sky and soared high with her captive. Canto begged incoherently, then screamed as her talon pierced his belly. The prince fell abruptly silent and drops of his blood fell like blue rain.

"She kept her word," the clerk acknowledged. "It *was* quick." Then he bowed his head and murmured a prayer.

Nero hastened down the stairs, knowing he had witnessed all he needed to see. He raced across the courtyard, composing his account in his mind. There was blue blood spattered over the Starpod, a blue so deep as to be nearly purple.

It was the unmistakable hue of the blood of the crown family of Regalia.

Nero spared a glance upward in time to see the princess bite into the prince and shake him like a doll. The way she tore at his flesh indicated that there would be nothing left of him.

Nothing but the word of Nero, the princess, and the clerk from Regalia.

Could he be relied upon?

The princess roared in that very moment. Nero looked up to see something gold falling toward him, catching the light as it spun ever downward. He snatched it out of the air, then opened his hand. It was the signet ring of the crown prince, the mark of his station and his inheritance.

Even Nero knew that the princes of Regalia never suffered to have the ring of state removed. It was eased from the royal finger after death, and not a moment before.

The ring, and the blue blood already drying upon it, told eloquently of what Nero had witnessed. He had to make haste back to Incendium.

When the Starpod settled gently into its parking spot at Incendium's star station Nero wanted to leap out and kiss the ground. He would be a happy man to never transport again.

He wasn't even sure he'd ride the sim.

But he recalled the decorum expected of those in the royal service. He left the vehicle with dignity, returning its wishes for a pleasant day, and thanked the attendant at the star station. A team hastily surrounded the vehicle and began to refuel it. He strode back toward the palace, intent upon giving his report to Kraw with all haste.

Nero immediately discovered why the Starpod might be in demand. He found the palace in uproar. Guests were leaving in droves—some, in fact, could have been said to be fleeing Incendium. The courtyard thronged with servants, each trying to summon the vehicle of choice for their lords and masters. The congestion was unholy. He could hear the booming commands of King Ouros, and the shrill notes of Queen Ignita as both strove to calm their guests.

Inside the palace, the chaos was even worse.

Servants ran up and down the great stairs, hustling and bustling. He heard complaints and a good bit of gossip. Some of the guests were on their comms, telling others of events on Incendium, and Kraw was nowhere to be seen.

Nero decided that the viceroy must be in the imperial chambers. He took a deep breath and dared to push his way up the stairs. He felt like one of the zarcota fish that traveled upstream to spawn each spring near Mola, for he was the only one trying to climb the stairs. The deluge of guests poured downward, heading to the courtyard and the starport. It was only with real determination—and probably because of some size advantage—that he made any progress at all.

He was surprised that so few of them chose to remain to eat. He could smell the feast that had been prepared, and his own belly growled at its emptiness. Surely the food wouldn't be wasted?

Nero reached the summit of the stairs and heard Kraw's voice. He was trying to soothe someone, probably the king or queen. He couldn't speak without an invitation in their presence. He would make himself visible, though, and hope to attract Kraw's attention. He gripped the signet ring and stepped into the royal chamber.

It was an astonishing room. Nero had seen it in hologram, of course, for all the great ceremonies of Incendium were held in this room and broadcast on the vid to the citizens of Incendium. In reality, it was far more glorious and much bigger than he'd imagined.

In this moment, it was almost empty, so its

marvels were easily appreciated. The chamber was still decorated for the exchange of vows, with flowers and garlands of flowers in every hue. Some of the garlands had been torn free of their moorings, and there were bright petals on the ground. More than one blossom had been crushed underfoot when the guests left.

On the far side of the chamber, near a pair of thrones, Kraw spoke to a couple. Even if Nero hadn't recognized King Ouros and Queen Ignita from their official images, the splendor of their garments and their crowns would have revealed their identity to him. The viceroy was speaking quickly. The king looked annoyed. The queen appeared to be flustered.

Nero fingered the ring. He stood politely, hoping Kraw's gaze would pass his way.

In the meantime, he looked. Glory of the stars, the floor was magnificent. It was a map of Incendium, wrought of a hundred colors of stones from the planet's mines, the surface polished to such a gleam that Nero could almost see his reflection in it.

But the ceiling stole his breath away. He wanted to sit down hard when he tipped back his head to look. It arched so high overhead, leaving plenty of space for the royal family to shift shape, of course. Even though he had read of its design and glimpsed it in the vid, the splendor of the depiction of the stars in the galaxy nearly made his mouth drop open in wonder. They were brighter and more clear than even during the darkest nights in Medior, far from the lights of the city.

It was magnificent even despite the large hole on one side of the ceiling, where the actual sky could be seen.

Nero guessed that the princess had departed that way.

A party of architects arrived and hastened to consult with Kraw. The viceroy turned his attention to them and drew King Ouros into the discussion. It was an artful choice, for the king immediately began planning the reconstruction. His anger dissipated as the architects discussed the challenges with him. Nero had read that the king had a particular interest in engineering and it was clear that he enjoyed the consultation and debate.

In the opposite corner, royal astrologers in their distinctive blue robes—the ones embroidered with stars and hemmed in fiery hues—argued over several horoscopes. The older one who had wanted to see his charts, the one who would have challenged him outright, looked up and glared at Nero.

Nero returned his gaze steadily. He had been right. He felt the older man's will and his malice and wondered at it.

Had Sapior known this man?

"Are you lost?" a woman asked from so close beside Nero that he jumped.

Nero spun, an explanation rising to his lips, then fell silent when he realized it was one of the crown princesses who addressed him. It was the youngest of the twelve, the princess Pericula, her long wavy copper hair hanging unbound over her shoulders. It fell almost to her knees, gleaming like a river. Her face was heart-shaped, her lips perfectly rosy, and her blue eyes sparkled as if they were filled with starlight.

Nero felt hot and then cold. She was beautiful.

He shouldn't have been surprised that she was more beautiful than her hologram.

His heart raced.

They called her Peri, he knew.

She *had* addressed him first.

Nero bowed low. "Highness!" He could see that her robe was of a midnight blue that favored her perfectly and there seemed to be gold threads woven into the cloth. It gleamed when she moved, catching the light, and was hemmed with white fur.

She laughed a little. "Rise," she commanded. "I didn't mean to frighten you."

Nero straightened and restrained the urge to tug at the hem of his tabard. He was woefully underdressed to be speaking to a princess, and not as fastidiously groomed as he would have preferred. He could feel the weight of the astrologer's glare. "I am not frightened, Highness."

Peri surveyed him. "I imagine not. You look as if you have been on an adventure," she said, and he heard unexpected yearning in her voice. Then she laughed and shook a finger at him. "Don't disappoint me by admitting otherwise."

Nero folded his hands behind his back, taking the posture of the architects who consulted with the king. "I had the honor to be dispatched by the viceroy to follow the princess Drakina."

Peri's eyes widened. "She went after Canto, didn't she? What happened?"

Nero showed her the signet ring and they both stared at it for a long moment of silence.

"This is very bad," she whispered.

Nero didn't think it prudent to agree.

Peri considered him. "You are courageous to bring such tidings to my father."

"It is only right, Highness, to fulfill the task I've been given."

"But valiant all the same." She surveyed him again, and he had a sense of her quick mind. "Why you?" She winced and he felt a commonality with her, for he was oft in the situation of speaking his mind and giving offense when he meant none. "I mean no insult, of course, but you are not in my father's livery. I would have expected him to send a clerk or a guard."

He shrugged. "Perhaps I was expendable."

"Never!" The glow in her eyes made his heart thump.

"Perhaps he thought it fitting to send me because I had brought an unwelcome prophecy."

Peri's smile faded and wonder lit her features. "*You* are an astrologer?"

Nero nodded, wondering why she doubted it.

"What was the prophecy?"

He pointed to the gaping hole in the roof.

"Truly?" Peri was clearly impressed. She indicated the court astrologers. "They didn't have a hint of it, and we were taken completely by surprise as a result." Her disdain was clear. "You must bring these tidings of Drakina's deed to my father."

King Ouros raised his voice again, his frustration having returned. Perhaps the repair would be more expensive than he might have hoped. Nero knew that the messenger might pay the price due for the message, but having Peri by his side made it imperative that he behave with courage.

"You advise correctly, Highness. I simply did not wish to interrupt."

"Of course. What is your name, astrologer?"

"Nero, Highness. From Mola."

"You journeyed all that way!" She sighed. "And seen half the world. I am envious."

Nero was shocked when Peri seized his elbow. Her touch was light, her hand small and fair. He had been touched by a princess, who had also spoken with him.

If his life ended in the next few moments, he would not consider it wasted.

"Father!" she called. Kraw and the royal pair turned to look. "This man returns from Kraw's quest with tidings." The architects fell silent and faced Nero. "His name is Nero and he is an astrologer."

A man cleared his throat, and Nero saw that the astrologers had trailed behind them. "He is no astrologer, Highness," the old one said in an indulgent tone. "For he has not studied at—much less graduated from—the Royal University for Astrologers."

Peri turned a glare upon him. "Yet he foresaw this day's outcome as you did not," she said, her tone scathing. "I would suggest, Father, that you add Nero to your advisors. His loyalty is beyond question. He journeyed alone all the way from Mola to tell you of this, then immediately followed Drakina as Kraw bade him."

"But what tidings," Kraw demanded, stepping forward. "What did the princess do?"

Nero held out his hand, Canto's signet ring cradled in his palm.

Kraw paled, then plucked the ring from Nero's palm.

King Ouros' eyes flashed fire. "She will cast us to war!"

Nero didn't think it wise to suggest that the princess had tried to mitigate the damage. "My chart, Highness, does indicate a tribunal court finding in her favor."

"The chart that he will not let any of us examine," the astrologer sniffed.

"The chart that was right when you were wrong," Peri retorted.

"The chart I did not learn about in time!" Ouros roared. "I will hear no more of this on this day!" The King of Incendium shifted shape in a blaze of light. He leapt into the air and flew in a tight circle high in the royal chamber, then shot through the hole in the roof to rage fire at the sky.

"It will be good for him," Queen Ignita said, sighing then squaring her shoulders. "Ouros is no diplomat, to be sure. Kraw, you must send an official apology to Queen Arcana. The negotiations will be difficult, though perhaps you can suggest this notion of a tribunal court to her."

"Of course, Highness."

"I leave the matter in your capable hands."

Kraw bowed, then cast Nero a glance. "And the astrologer from Mola?"

"Has served us better in a mere day than many who have been sworn to the house for far longer," Ignita said, steel in her tone. "He will join the royal astrologers, if that is his will."

Nero's heart leapt and he was well aware of Peri's pleasure. "It is, Highness. I thank you for this honor."

The oldest astrologer again protested. "Highness, I would not challenge your choice, but I think it ill-advised. You know full well, Highness, that all of the royal astrologers have completed a rigorous program of study at the university. This man is unknown to us."

"And perhaps his route of education provides new insights," Ignita countered smoothly. "He will be *my* astrologer, Kraw, for I need one who tells me even unwelcome truths."

"Of course, Highness," Kraw and the astrologers said in unison, bowing deeply.

The queen arched a fair brow. "Does this displease you, Nero of Mola?"

"No, Highness. I am simply astonished to have my dream come true with such haste."

Queen Ignita laughed. "Then you must dream bigger, Nero of Mola." She extended her hand imperiously and he fell to one knee, bowing his head as he kissed the ring on her finger.

When the queen retreated and the viceroy hastened to do her will, Nero found himself alone again with the princess Peri. "You are both valiant and clever, it is clear," she said, approval in her tone. "You did not hesitate at all, or tremble in the royal presence. That is not common amongst new arrivals."

"I did only my duty, Highness." Nero dared to smile at her, and her lips curved in response.

"You did more," she murmured, her eyes shining so brilliantly that his heart leapt. Their gazes clung for a potent moment, one in which Nero found it hard to breathe. "I look forward to learning more of you, Nero of Mola," she said, then offered her hand in turn.

Nero bent deeply again. He would have kissed her ring, but Peri did not wear any gems on her fingers. He was compelled, then, to touch his lips to her skin, and he certainly didn't mind. Her hand was soft and faintly perfumed, but he saw strength in her fingers. She could be a warrior princess if she so chose, just like her sister, but he didn't fear her. Her heart would guide her true.

"I thank you, Highness," he said and she leaned down to whisper to him.

"When we are alone, call me Peri."

Peri. Nero's heart stopped cold, rather than exploding as he'd feared.

He looked left and right, but they were alone. "I will do so, Peri, at your command."

She smiled, her eyes dancing with an enticing mischief. "Will you cast my horoscope first?" she whispered.

"I should be delighted, Highness." At her sharp look, Nero cleared his throat. "Peri," he corrected, and she laughed. "The task will take some time."

"Of course. Neither of us is leaving the palace, Nero. Please take all the time you require."

He bowed again, amazed that she seemed to feel regret in parting from him.

"I would know the identity of my HeartKeeper, Nero."

"I shall endeavor to discern it." He swallowed. "Peri."

Her smile made his heart thunder. "My mother awaits me. Farewell for the moment, Nero."

And then Peri was gone, hastening across the hall on light feet, her glittering robe flowing behind her. Her hair shone and he heard her laughter as she conferred with her mother.

Dream bigger.

Nero felt a new yearning light in his heart. Queen Ignita's advice was remarkably easy to take.

One thing was certain: the horoscope he drew for Peri would be the most beautiful and the most careful one he had ever done. Who was the man who would claim her heart forever? Nero could only hope the man in question was worthy of the lady.

The princess was not the only one curious as to what her future held.

Watch for

WYVERN'S PRINCE

Book 2 in the Dragons of Incendium series

Coming Soon!

The Dragons of Incendium have their own website
http://dragonsofincendium.com

Books by Deborah Cooke

Paranormal Romances:
The Dragonfire Series
Kiss of Fire
Kiss of Fury
Kiss of Fate
Harmonia's Kiss
Winter Kiss
Whisper Kiss
Darkfire Kiss
Flashfire
Ember's Kiss
The Dragon Legion Collection
Serpent's Kiss
Firestorm Forever

The Dragons of Incendium
Wyvern's Mate
Nero's Dream
Wyvern's Prince (2016)
Wyvern's Warrior (2016

Paranormal Young Adult:
The Dragon Diaries
Flying Blind
Winging It
Blazing the Trail

Contemporary Romance:
The Coxwells
Third Time Lucky
Double Trouble
One More Time
All or Nothing

Flatiron Five
Simply Irresistible (June 2016)

Books by Claire Delacroix

Time Travel Romances
Once Upon a Kiss
The Last Highlander
The Moonstone
Love Potion #9

Historical Romances
The Romance of the Rose
Honeyed Lies
Unicorn Bride
The Sorceress
Roarke's Folly
Pearl Beyond Price
The Magician's Quest
Unicorn Vengeance
My Lady's Champion
Enchanted
My Lady's Desire

The Bride Quest
The Princess
The Damsel
The Heiress
The Countess
The Beauty
The Temptress

The Rogues of Ravensmuir
The Rogue
The Scoundrel
The Warrior

The Jewels of Kinfairlie
The Beauty Bride
The Rose Red Bride
The Snow White Bride
The Ballad of Rosamunde

Deborah Cooke sold her first book in 1992, a medieval romance called **The Romance of the Rose** published under her pseudonym Claire Delacroix. Since then, she has published over fifty novels in a wide variety of sub-genres, including historical romance, contemporary romance, paranormal romance, fantasy romance, time-travel romance, women's fiction, paranormal young adult and fantasy with romantic elements. She has published under the names Claire Delacroix, Claire Cross, and Deborah Cooke. **The Beauty**, part of her successful Bride Quest series of historical romances, was her first title to land on the *New York Times* List of Bestselling Books. Her books routinely appear on other bestseller lists and have won numerous awards. In 2009, she was the writer-in-residence at the Toronto Public Library, the first time the library has hosted a residency focused on the romance genre. In 2012, she was honored to receive the Romance Writers of America's Mentor of the Year Award.

Currently, she writes paranormal romances and contemporary romances under the name Deborah Cooke. She also writes medieval romances as Claire Delacroix. Deborah lives in Canada with her husband and family, as well as far too many unfinished knitting projects.

For more information about Deborah's books, please visit her website at

http://deborahcooke.com

Printed in Poland
by Amazon Fulfillment
Poland Sp. z o.o., Wro